Freak Show

Part 1: By Its Cover

KRISTOPHER MCCLENDON

authorHOUSE®

AuthorHouse™
1663 Liberty Drive
Bloomington, IN 47403
www.authorhouse.com
Phone: 1 (800) 839-8640

The following work contains elements of satire. Similarities to actual persons
and events are coincidental. None of the content is an accurate representation
of the world or the views of the author, publisher, or retailer.

Published by AuthorHouse   10/04/2017

ISBN: 978-1-5246-7269-0 (sc)
ISBN: 978-1-5246-7268-3 (e)

Print information available on the last page.

This book is printed on acid-free paper.

CHAPTER 1

Ḣere Comes the Carnival

IT WAS afternoon on a cloudless day in the city of New Wayton. There was an empty lot bordered with cement walls. The ground was covered in dirt and autumn leaves that blew around in the cool wind.

Two girls entered the lot wearing strange clothes. The oldest looked to be around fifteen. She had black hair and brown eyes, and she wore the strangest clothes of the two. She wore a black leather coat with coattails, black gloves, a red skirt, black and white-striped long socks, black shoes with a copper buckle, and to top it off, she was adorned with a top hat. Her attire seemed to resemble that of a stage magician with her own twist added to it.

She was looking at a flyer in her hands. "Future site of the New Wayton Bank," she read. "Not anymore," she said with a smirked and tossed the paper into the wind. "Isn't that right, Dodie?" the girl asked her young companion.

Eight-year-old Dodie had cotton candy pink hair. She had cold, emerald eyes, and she wore businesslike attire: a white shirt with a small brown tie, khaki shorts, and brown shoes. In her arms she held a laptop. She was drumming away at the keys.

"Done," Dodie said. "The carnival now owns this lot. However, there'll no doubt be suspicion about us, Janette."

Janette scoffed at this remark. "It's not like they could do anything."

With that she took off her hat, reached into it, and took out what appeared to be a blue jack-in-the-box decorated with gold stars. She tossed the toy on the ground where it rolled toward the center of the lot and began playing music as its handle turned on its own.

Janette performed a bit of jive as she listened to the tune while Dodie rolled her eyes at this foolishness. When the song finished, the box sprang open and a dark cloud erupted from the toy, draping the area in a dark veil. As the smoke subsided, a large circus tent stood before them.

Janette heaved an exaggerated sigh. "Whew, I'm beat."

"Sarcastic as always," Dodie replied with an annoyed tone.

Just then a young, dark-haired woman walked in carrying brightly colored luggage that went with her outrageous outfit.

She wore a one-piece black outfit with transparent leggings, red heels, black gloves, rabbit ear accessories, and large white sunglasses. The woman gasped and dropped her luggage at the sight of the tent.

"Oh my gosh, it's perfect," she cried as she removed her white sunglasses to get a better look at the tent. In doing so, she revealed her light brown eyes.

"Mimi, where were you?" Dodie asked, staring at the heaps of luggage.

"So ... when do we perform?" Mimi asked, completely blowing her off. Janette smiled deviously. "Soon."

Janette took another small toy box out of her hat and placed it on the ground. The three girls backed away from this box when Janette snapped her fingers. As if on command, the box grew, and a rumbling sound came from within. The box began to shake as if something was trying to get out. The box became the size of a shipping crate when the door flew open, releasing a stir-crazy mob of circus clowns and performers from its interior.

The clowns cheered and giggled childishly as they hurriedly entered the tent. Just then a police officer pulled into the parking lot and made his way to the lot to investigate this circus tent that had suddenly sprung up.

"Hey!" the man called as he entered the stolen lot.

"I told you," Dodie said.

"What's all this?" the officer asked as he walked up to the three girls.

"Why, it's a circus," Janette replied sarcastically.

The officer gave her a dirty look. "Funny. Do you guys have permission?"

Dodie spoke up: "Actually, we own this lot."

"Yeah, well last I checked this was owned by the bank," the officer retorted.

"Then you weren't paying attention," Dodie smack-talked, trying to sound superior.

"Right. I want to see your manager. Wait a sec ... Shouldn't you kids be in school?" the officer asked.

Janette spoke up. "School is for losers, and I run this gig."

The officer was about to speak when Mimi jumped into the conversation.

"Why hello, officer, Is there anything I can help you with?" She flirted while batting her eyelashes as she struck a pose to show off her curvature.

The officer was taken aback by her sudden appearance. "What the heck are you wearing?"

Mimi giggled. "Do you like it?"

"Cute," the officer replied before pushing Mimi aside, leaving her in a foul mood.

"Is she your mother?" the officer asked Dodie, pointing to Mimi. Dodie gagged at this question.

"So where's your boss?" the officer continued.

"I'm the boss," Janette restated.

"Don't play games with me," the officer demanded, wanting to be shown some respect.

"Really, you're the one playing the game. I keep telling you I run this place. You just refuse to listen," Janette replied with a smirk.

"If you don't cooperate, I will have no choice but to take you in," the officer threatened.

Janette said, "You do have a choice. You just choose not to listen because it will make you look bad. The first priority of every officer is to look like a badass when they are merely children wanting to feel special. But nothing about them is special," lecturing him without batting an eye.

Naturally the cop was insulted and infuriated at having his own reasons and personality brought into question. He wouldn't admit it, even if it was true. The adult thing to do, after all, was to look superior.

"Cheeky brat, I'm taking all of you down to the station," he grumbled and reached for Janette in a fit of rage.

With that, Janette's eyes briefly darkened for a split second as if reacting to the hostility. Janette jumped backward a significant distance without much effort as she snapped her fingers. As if on command, the walls of an iron cage flipped out of clouds of smoke from the ground. The officer yelped in shock and grasped the bars in his hand to see if they were real.

Janette began to walk around the cage. "Now you see ... I don't feel like going anywhere with you."

"Let me out of this cage or else!" the officer threatened.

Janette smirked. "Or else what? You're going to wave your police badge at me? It's just a piece of metal, and it doesn't mean crap." The officer reached for his walkie-talkie and began to request help from the station.

"Sorry, the number you dialed isn't available. Please call again later. Maybe then we will actually care to reply," Janette's voice replied from the walkie-talkie.

The officer was astounded. Janette hadn't opened her mouth at all. Janette shrugged her shoulders as if she didn't know anything.

The officer reached for his gun only to have his hand be blasted by a ball of fire. The officer cried in pain as he held his hand that turned red and began to blister. Fear kicked in when he realized he was now like a caged animal.

The officer started stuttering. "Who are you? Wh-what's wrong with you people?"

Janette extinguished the flame burning in her and nonchalantly replied, "We're people, so … that would be everything."

Dodie spoke up, irritated by Janette's behavior. "Oh, Miss Janette person—do you mind speeding this game of yours along? We have work to do."

"Okay, okay. Well, Mr. Officer, enjoy your new life."

With that Janette took out a small handkerchief and threw it into the air where it became a large drape that covered the cage.

"Let me out!" the officer screamed. Lights and purple smoke emitted from behind the drape. The silhouette of the officer changed with each flash, and the rumbling of thunder came from behind the curtain.

With that the cage collapsed, revealing a small brown dog that took the officer's place. The dog looked around and whimpered as it realized what had happened.

"An animal this time?" Dodie asked curiously.

"He was annoying," Janette said in defense.

Mimi's face contorted with disgust. Her skin crawled as she stamped her feet and screamed, "Eew! Dog!" The dog looked up at her, wondering what was going to happen to him.

With that, Mimi brought her foot back and punted the dog with superhuman strength out of the lot. The dog yelped as it went over the wall and landed with a thud on the other side. This act astonished Dodie and Janette.

"I hate dogs. They're gross and dirty," Mimi said to justify her action, shivering at the mere thought of having touched one.

"I'm sure the dog is dead now, so don't worry about it anymore. Anyway, back to business." Dodie said.

"We can do that later. What we need to do now is celebrate." Janette said, smiling as she made her way to the tent.

"Celebrate?" Dodie asked as if this were a foreign word.

"Celebrating my … I mean *our* debut. What else would it be?" Mimi replied as they followed Janette into the tent.

The clowns were all around, performing all manner of stunts and shenanigans atop bleachers, tightropes, and acrobat swings as the three girls entered. Janette made her way to the center ring and climbed up an elevated pedestal. She took out a microphone and whistled, sending an eardrum-shattering sound throughout the complex.

All the clowns stopped in their tracks and gathered around like children for story time. "Ladies and gentle-freaks," Janette announced. "I'm here to announce the official opening of our Shadow Carnival." The crowd responded with a deafening cheer and applause. Janette signaled them to quiet down so she could continue. "And to celebrate this momentous occasion, I hereby declare that we start each workday with a song."

Dodie looked at her in bewilderment. "A song?"

"Yes, a song," Janette repeated.

"Oh, are we going to sing it now?" Mimi asked, bouncing in excitement. Janette threw her the microphone and took a second mike out of her hat.

"Hello, Shadow Carnival. Ready to be bewitched by my song?" Mimi asked seductively.

"You aren't seriously doing this are you?" Dodie asked, but was completely ignored as they started their cute and slightly disturbed song.

The two of them sang together: "Freaks, freaks, everyone's a freak. Freaks, freaks, isn't that neat? Freaks, freaks, a world with just freaks. Freaks, freaks, a world that can't be beat."

Janette soloed: "We are told that looks don't matter, but we don't like those who are fatter, those who are flatter. We are told not to be so vain, yet the men have muscle pain. What's the point to being so vain? When you're old, there's nothing to gain."

Dodie pinched her forehead and gave a heavy sigh. They repeated the "Freaks" verse, and the crowd sang along with them while Dodie left to find a quiet spot.

Janette soloed once more: "When we're young, we want to be adults, but so many are nasty cutthroats. It shouldn't be about who is right, but when they are wrong, they scream and fight. If you think this is just a bunch of shit, then you are a worthless hypocrite."

After another return to the "Freaks" verse, Mimi and Janette both sang: "Oh have pity on the spoiled youth, For they are blind to the real truth. They are not who they wish to be, simply avoiding reality. All wrapped up in filthy lies, the spoiled youth ... might as well die,"

"Freaks, freaks, everyone's a freak. Freaks, freaks, isn't that neat? Freaks, freaks, a world with just freaks. Freaks, freaks, a world that can never, ever be beat."

Janette finished the song and the crowd cheered. Mimi blew kisses to the crowd and waved as if she were the only performer, while Janette tipped her hat with a smug look on her face.

So having set up their tent, murdered a police officer, and sung their daily theme song, the Shadow Carnival had settled into their new home. The city of New Wayton was a big place. It would take a lot of work to shake up the city. After all, who else was there to spread mayhem?

CHAPTER 2

An Average Day

A RED-HAIRED TEACHER named Ms. Heckle stood in the front of a crowded classroom, sprawling the agenda for the day on the whiteboard with fruit-scented markers. The students chatted in hushed tones—or what they thought was hushed—and busily text messaged each other as they childishly hid their phones under the desk so they wouldn't look suspicious.

Ms. Heckle looked out the window and saw a gray sky while drops of rain began to splatter against the glass. After writing the subject of the day on the board, she closed the shutters as if it would help and returned to her desk to begin passing a fire extinguisher on the way.

"All right, you know the drill: No talking and put your phones away." Ms. Heckle grumbled as she opened up the nearest textbook.

"Now … who can tell me about the colonies?" Ms. Heckle asked as the class fell silent. One student sheepishly raised her hand. Ms. Heckle sighed as if this was to be expected.

"Did anyone besides Peggie read the chapter?" she asked sarcastically.

Everyone was silent. Young, black pigtailed, blue-eyed Peggie kept her hand raised. Ms. Heckle rolled her eyes and called on the only diligent student.

"Colonists opened trade routes with England for goods," Peggie answered.

"What did they trade?" Ms. Heckle asked. Peggie took a moment to think.

"I think they traded furs and animal pelts."

Satisfied, Ms. Heckle replied, "They did trade with the natives for those, so I suppose that is correct." She instructed everyone to turn to some three-digit page number in their behemoth of a textbook. As Peggie eagerly did so, she overheard the gossiping of students.

"She's such a showoff," one student muttered under her breath.

"She probably thinks we're stupid," the other replied. Peggie felt a twinge of pain in her chest.

"You all better be paying attention. This will be on the test," Ms. Heckle said, grabbing everyone's attention again. "Moving into some local history: The town of Old Wayton was founded in 1621," she began the lecture, circling the year 1621 in red.

The class continued until the lunch bell dinged over the intercom. The students instantly jumped out of their seats and made their way out of the class like a pack of well-trained dogs. Peggie casually packed her things and headed into the crowded hallway, the last person to leave. She navigated her way through the rushing torrent of human bodies and strolled into the colorful cafeteria where she looked around at all the food stands. Eventually she decided to get a cheap chicken sandwich and waited in line as if she were at an amusement park on opening day.

As she waited, a boy her age joined the line. "Hey, Pegs," he said in greeting.

"Oh, hi, Zack," she replied to the shaggy-brown-haired, brown-eyed boy.

"Are you doing anything this weekend?" Zack asked as they moved along the line.

"Not really. I have to help out with the play on the weekend."

"So you're doing the extra credit too?" Zack asked, surprised.

"Oh, so you're helping out too?" Peggie replied, surprised and relieved to hear this.

"Yeah, didn't do too well on that math test," he answered, depressed about being robbed of his weekend. "I never thought finding the shaded area of a circle would be that difficult."

Just then a tall, brown ponytailed girl in a long-sleeved shirt pushed Peggie out of the way, cutting in line.

"What the … Hey!" Peggie squeaked in surprise.

"What?" the girl replied with a scornful glare.

"Y-you can't do that. I … I was here first," Peggie stuttered.

"So what?" the girl said, mocking Peggie.

"Knock it off, Sal. Wait in line like everyone else," Zack ordered in defense.

"I'm already in line, idiot," Sal insisted.

"Don't make me get security on you," Zack threatened. Everyone in line stared as if a large-screen TV had been introduced to bunch of children. Sal towered over him, crossing her brutishly large arms.

"What, can't do anything yourself?"

"Just let her go, Zack," Peggie cautioned, hidden safely behind him.

"You can't let her treat you like that," Zack growled.

Sal's eyes fixated on Peggie. Sal grinned fiendishly, showing teeth so yellow they could glow in the dark.

"Besides, we're close to the front anyway," Peggie said reasonably but sounding depressed as she looked at the floor.

"Why, Peggie?" Zack mumbled.

"I thought so," Sal said, gloating over her victory.

After getting their lunch, the two scoured the area, strolling along the rows of blue tables. They finally found a small table that was free by the bulletin board and sat down. Peggie just wanted to forget what had happened, but Zack was furious.

"Why did you let her go?" Zack asked, popping a potato fry into his mouth.

Setting her pink backpack on the floor, Peggie said, "Well ..." She grabbed the sandwich and took a bite to stall. Zack rolled his eyes and asked again as soon as she was done chewing.

"I ... I didn't want to get into trouble," she stuttered meekly, staring at her tray.

"But you didn't do anything wrong. Why would you get in trouble?" he asked, puzzled by this nonsensical statement. Peggie bit her lip as she glanced at the floor.

Zack sighed and relaxed. "Whatever."

"I'm sorry. It's not like I wanted to. I just ... I just can't. I don't know why," Peggie said apologetically.

Zack glanced over the cluttered message board, covered with all sorts of announcements. Among the disorganized mess of papers was a section that listed missing persons.

"School started just a few weeks ago. Now students are missing? What is the world coming to?" Zack thought out loud as he looked over the pictures of the students.

Peggie looked up and noticed the picture of a hefty girl with short, black hair and brown eyes, forcing a fake smile on her freckled face. She said, "I remember seeing that girl at the beginning of school. It's hard to believe that someone I know would just disappear like that."

Zack crossed his arms, pondering this rash of disappearances. "It's all over the news, too. I heard even a police officer is missing. It appears to be kidnapping."

Peggie took a sip out of the miniature milk carton. "I sure hope nothing like that happens again. I wouldn't know what to do if one of my friends went missing. It would be even scarier if it happened to me."

"Just don't do anything stupid, and you should be okay. You know the basic rules, right?" Zack said to comfort Peggie.

Peggie thought back to her elementary school days. "Like not going with strangers?"

"That and always staying where there's a lot of people. Crooks won't do anything where there are a lot of witnesses and people to stop them. Plus it makes it hard to pick someone out. When it comes down to it, they're really afraid of being caught."

"I see," Peggie said, disturbed by the thought of being abducted.

Zack saw that she was getting worried, so he changed the subject. "Hey, I'll be working at the TV station in a couple of weeks." Peggie's jaw dropped.

"Really? What will you be doing?" she asked.

Zack blushed. "It's not much, but I'll get to voice act one or two lines for a side character in a cartoon."

"No way," Peggie said.

"It's true. It's just a character that no one will ever see again, so my dad suggested I go for it." Zack said, smirking.

"Your dad is like what? One of the managers, right? Can he do that?" Peggie asked.

"Gosh, Peggie it's not a crime or anything. Besides, I want to see how that stuff is made."

"So you really do want to make cartoons?"

Zack shook his head and replied, "I could, but I'm not sure yet."

"Why not? Those flipbooks you make are really good," she said to encourage him while recalling the image of a cat chasing a bird.

"They're not *that* good," he replied humbly.

At that moment Sal came and sat at their table. The two were so shocked by her abruptness that they didn't stop her from taking Peggie's tray.

"What the hell are you doing, Sal?" Zack said with a growl.

"Hey, give me my food!" Peggie demanded.

"*Your* food? If you're that hungry, go wait in line," the girl said with a smirk and began to wolf down what was left of the chicken sandwich.

"That's it." Zack shouted angrily and stormed off.

"What are you gonna do about it?" Sal asked. Her intimidating stare turned into a grin when Zack left.

Peggie wondered why he left. She began to feel abandoned but was reassured when Zack came back with a woman wearing a black shirt with the word *Security* emblazoned across her back, a communication device at her side, and a scary look on her face.

Sal's jaw dropped at the sight of this woman towering over her, looking down upon her as if she could be stepped on at any moment.

"What seems to be the problem here?" the woman asked sternly.

Sal pointed a finger at Peggie and quickly spouted the first thing that popped into her head. "W-well you see, she thinks this is her sandwich." Peggie's jaw dropped on hearing this blatant lie.

"Oh, so you must be the girl who hasn't been paying for her meals. Give her the sandwich ... *now!*" the woman commanded, crossing her arms, leaving Sal at a loss for words.

As the security guard escorted her to the office, Sal looked back and glared hatefully at Peggie. Zack returned to his seat with a beaming smile on his face.

Peggie just stared at him in bewilderment. "Y-you actually got security on her?"

"Duh. It's their job, and you can't let her get away with that."

Peggie looked away and muttered under her breath, "Why can't I do that?"

As the school day continued, the events that happened at lunch hung over Peggie like a rain cloud. Seeing Zack's display of courage left her feeling ashamed and powerless in comparison.

The remainder of the classes served as a petty distraction. The day ended with an announcement from the principal, Mr. Bernsley: "All students: Due to the increase of disappearances, the faculty will escort students to the busses. Also, no one may leave the campus to walk home alone. Please have someone walk with you."

Everyone rushed out the door as soon as the announcements were over. But Peggie once again took her time leaving. She walked down the checkered hallway past the gymnasium, walked onto the pavement, and got in line to board the bus. The humming of the engines was overpowered by chattering students, and the smell of exhaust filled the air. Peggie climbed into the bus and took a seat by the window. Sal followed her on and sat on the seat across from her. The bus finally pulled out, but Peggie was unaware of the heated and hateful glare Sal was giving her.

CHAPTER 3

Opening Act

WHEN THE doors of the school bus folded and slid open, the students all crammed their way onto the narrow walkway. Peggie patiently waited for the chaos to settle. Sal watched the line closely, scanning students as if she had set up a security checkpoint at an airport.

Peggie followed the back of the line. Her eyes met Sal, who grinned mischievously. Sal got behind Peggie, followed her off the bus, and said, "Hey, Peggie, let me talk to you for a sec."

Peggie looked back briefly but tried to ignore her as she followed the other students down the street. When the bus drove off, Sal rushed at Peggie, pulled on the back of her shirt, dragged her behind the brick wall of the building, and stared at her intimidatingly.

"Wh-what do you want?" Peggie asked with her back against the cold, hard, rigid wall.

"I didn't like how you got me in trouble. What are you going to do about it?" Sal demanded with her nostrils flaring.

Peggie was confused. "What do you mean?"

"You told your friend to get me in trouble, didn't you?" Sal stamped her foot like a child.

"But I didn't."

"Don't lie to me."

"I'm sorry."

"That won't cut it. I want your money." Sal stuck out her palm.

"What?" Peggie asked, gasping.

"You heard me. Hand it over!"

"But I already spent it."

"You have leftover change don't you?"

"But it's in my account." Peggie's eyes welled up, and she cried.

Sal curled her hand into a fist. "Then get me some," she ordered. Peggie closed her eyes just as the sound of someone clapping broke the mood. Sal turned around to see a strange girl giggling. It was Janette from the Shadow Carnival.

"The classic lunch scheme? Oh, that never gets old." Janette held her stomach, laughed, and hunched over as if afflicted by some disease.

Sal was infuriated. "What's so funny?" Janette calmed herself and pretended to wipe away a tear.

"Why, you of course. Who *else* would I be laughing at? I mean, lunch money? Come on, what a cliché." Janette said, taunting Sal.

"Damn freak. You want some, too?" Sal bellowed.

Janette grinned. "What an interesting choice of words. But I think you're mistaken about who the real freak is … or rather will be."

"What'd you say?" Sal screamed, towering over the odd girl. Janette's eyes changed colors to something unnatural: her pupils turned pure black with a pearl-like sheen to them, and her irises became pure white. You couldn't help but stare into the attention-drawing white rings.

Janette next spoke extra clearly, intending to wound Sal. "What I'm saying is … you're a nuisance. Ever since you were born, you've been nothing but a burden to take care of, and the moment you turn eighteen it'll be out on the streets with you. After all, it's your fault everything in your father's life is shit. The crime that you have committed is your very existence. That's why you're despised. That's why everyone is against you. That's why you're always in trouble: No one wants you. You were never meant to exist. You're nothing but a mistake. Nothing you ever do will change that."

Sal's mouth was agape with shock, and she quickly became extremely defensive.

"Sh-shut up! That isn't true." She screamed frantically, trying to retain her threatening presence, which was quickly evaporating.

"Good-for-nothing accident," Janette teased childishly in a sing-song voice.

"Shut up!" Sal said. Like a savage animal, she threw a punch at Janette, who merely blocked it with … her hat? Yes, it looked as if Janette's hat had eaten Sal's fist as it sank into the darkness within it.

Peggie watched with her mouth agape while Sal was rendered immobile by utter shock. Sal attempted to pull out her arm, but felt as if was wedged into a small hole. She began to pull on her arm with all her strength, becoming frantic from this nonsense.

Janette made a pouty face. Her eyes returned to their natural color as she babied Sal. "Aw, looks like you can't do anything."

"Sh-shut up! Let me go!" Sal stuttered and tried to punch with her other fist. With a wave of Janette's hand, Sal was lifted into the air as if there were invisible strings tied to her. With another hand gesture, Sal soon found herself on her back and dropped to the ground.

Sal was once again bewildered and confused as she lay on the grass. Janette casually strolled up, released Sal's arm, and reclaimed her hat. Peggie remained speechless at the sight of this strange girl. Sal got up and, with a wavering voice, tried to intimidate the girl. "Y-you better leave, if-if you know what's good for you."

"Looks like I don't, then." Janette played her threat off. Peggie was shocked to see the expression on Sal's face: She was one scared girl. Sal fell silent as she tried to figure out what to do next.

"Aw … you don't know what to do now? You're one nasty little girl. I know just what to do with you." Janette grinned as she snapped her fingers. Magically, a cage formed around Sal.

"Wh-what are you doing?" Sal murmured.

"Oh, nothing much. It's not like you're going to be any different than you are now. In fact it might even be an improvement. It's not like anyone would miss you. So ... bye-bye." Janette callously replied. She removed a handkerchief from her sleeve, threw it in the air, and draped it over the cage as it increased in size.

"What are you doing? Let me out." Sal began screaming from inside the cage when smoke billowed and lights flashed. The crashing of thunder was heard as if Sal was caged within a storm cloud. Her silhouette took on an odd appearance. As the screaming stopped, the cage collapsed, the smoke cleared, and Sal was left on her knees, dressed in a PE uniform, wearing obnoxiously large red boxing gloves. Janette smiled at the result of her work.

"What did you do?" Peggie finally asked, startling Janette.

"Oh ... I forgot all about you. Oh well, I guess it works out after all. I have to wait an hour anyway." Janette casually replied. She got behind Sal, pulled out a fold-up director's chair from her hat, and sat in the chair.

Peggie was horribly confused. "What are you talking about? An hour? What does that mean?" Suddenly Sal sprung up to her feet.

"Hi, boys and girls. It's me—Sally Sock'em." Sal threw a fist into the air as if she were some sort of character on a kid's show. She grinned and her face was covered in white face paint. One of her eyes was doused in black paint like it was bruised.

Peggie's jaw dropped, "Wh-what?" She gasped at this insane sight.

"Peggie!" Sal suddenly shouted and began bouncing on her feet, assuming some cheesy boxing pose.

"What?" Peggie replied without thinking.

"Your evil ends here, foul deceiver. I shall slay you where you stand." Sally proclaimed.

"What? Why? What are you talking about?" Peggie responded, very frightened.

Sal continued as if she were reciting the lines of a superhero from a show. "You claim ignorance? You and your henchmen framed me for a crime. Your trickery shall not be forgiven. I will beat a confession out of you to clear my name."

Peggie screamed as she moved out of the way of Sal's fist. She slammed it against the corner of the wall, knocking a large chunk of brick out of it and leaving a gaping crater where Peggie's head once was. Peggie continued screaming as she ran down the street.

"Hey! You're gonna get me in trouble again, aren't you? I won't let you hurt me. I won't let anyone hurt me." Sal chased after her while Janette laughed in the distance.

"Someone help! Please!" Peggie begged, but Sal quickly caught up.

"Here I go," Sal cheered and wound up for another attack. Peggie curled up into a ball and ducked out of the way, causing Sal to trip over her. The two girls tumbled onto the pavement, but they quickly got up and began running, Sal in pursuit.

Peggie wielded her backpack and in a desperate attempt took a swing at Sal. The heavy textbooks hit Sal's face, knocking her into a trash can.

"Leave me alone," Peggie screamed at her. She was about to dart off when unexpectedly, Sal began to cry.

Sal's eyes flickered like a television with bad reception. "I'm sorry, Daddy, I won't do it again, I promise." Peggie was confused by this behavior but received a flash of insight when she caught a glimpse of Sal's bruised arm.

Peggie was about pay the price of standing there like an idiot. Sal sprung up and gave Peggie a sharp jab to the stomach, causing her to collapse on the ground. Peggie was slow to get up. The throbbing pain in her stomach caused her body to shake when she attempted to get back on her feet. However, Sal kicked Peggie in the shoulder and then sat on top of her.

Peggie stared into the flickering TV static that filled Sal's eyes. A fiendish grin stretched across Sal's face.

Peggie's heart pounded as she pleaded: "Let me go, please." Peggie took a sudden blow to her cheek. Blood rushed into her cheek because it stung from the blow. "Does it feel good? Huh? *Does it?*" Sal screamed, punching her again in the eye and breaking Peggie's glasses.

Janette giggled at this scene. Her eyes once again changed to that odd appearance. Black smoke rose faintly from the ground around her as if small invisible fires were circling her. Janette wafted the fumes of these invisible fires. She took a deep breath and drew the smoke into her nostrils. Her body tingled, and she felt a surge of energy flow through her. Her mouth turned into a satisfied smile, and she exhaled with ecstasy.

"Oh how I do enjoy the scent of suffering." she commented, continuing to watch Peggie be tormented by her attacker.

"Stop her please!" Peggie cried. She took another blow that bent the frames of her glasses and scattered the remains of her lenses. Peggie felt a warm liquid begin to gush from her nose, and she let out a cry when she got hit again. Her nose was uncomfortably bent and no longer fit on her face. It was like wearing the wrong size shoe.

Janette giggled and then half-heartedly commanded: "Well, if you say so. Sal stop."

"No! She hurt me. I can't let anyone get away with that." Sal screamed at Janette, who shrugged her shoulders.

"I tried," Janette casually replied. She shrugged her shoulders as if she were innocent.

Peggie was in tears. She wanted it to stop, but it seemed as if no one was around.

"Suck it up and stop crying!" Sal screamed some more, raising her fist for another blow only to get pulled off of Peggie by some mysterious force.

"Hey, who did that?" Sal demanded furiously.

Peggie was yanked to her feet by what felt like someone pulling her arm. Peggie gasped at this and grew even more afraid. She couldn't see if anyone was there. Between her poor eyesight and one injured eye, it was almost impossible to make out the blurred objects in her surroundings.

"Don't worry. Just keep thinking about wanting to make her stop, and I'll handle the rest," a young female voice encouraged, as Peggie's arm was pulled again.

"Ah ha! I see you want more, don't you? Well then, I'll give you more." Sal howled as she charged. Peggie was freaking out, but before she knew it, a sudden cold sensation had taken over her hand, and a geyser of thick white mist spewed forth from her palm.

Sal yelped upon being pushed back by the force of this stream of mist. Her body temperature rapidly dropped, and numbness took over her limbs.

"H-hey, y-you're not su-supposed to do that," Sally whimpered. She wrapped her arms around herself and shivered when sheets of ice began clinging to her body.

Peggie just stared, completely stunned from shock. The invisible force had Peggie continue spewing more mist. Sal fell to her knees and her skin became pale. She held her head as if a head-splitting migraine had taken over. Sal cried in pain as her body flickered into a silhouette of TV static.

Sal screamed when her silhouette changed shape. As the television static faded, she collapsed onto the ground, unconscious this time, looking like her normal self. Peggie's legs gave out, and she fell to her knees with her heart pounding and butterflies in her stomach.

Janette finally got off her chair, tucked it back into her hat, and approached Sal. Janette's eyes return to normal during this quick journey. With a curious look, she inspected Sal as if she were a dead body at a crime scene. Janette looked back at Peggie with her mouth hanging open and began to crack up.

"I wasn't expecting that. Here I thought I would get no kind of resistance. If this is how it's going to go, I'll be happy to oblige," Janette said, cackling fiendishly.

Peggie was speechless on the whole matter. She stared at Janette as if she would explain something to her. Janette snapped her fingers, creating a cage around Sal once again.

Janette flew into the air and sat herself on top of the cage.

With an irritated tone, she explained briefly: "Since you look so pitiful right now, I'll go ahead and give you the short version. You've been recruited as a hero, so naturally that would make me the villain … again."

Peggie had begun to feel ill from an upset stomach. A slight hint of fever began to make itself known.

Janette let out an aggravated sigh, "I'll leave you alone for today. I have some big plans for this city that I need to prepare for." Janette's eyes momentarily changed again to black and white.

"So see you later, Princess Do Nothing," Janette heckled. With that final seemingly out-of-the-blue insult, Janette levitated the cage into the air and rode it into the sky.

Peggie collapsed and began crying from her traumatic experience. She just wanted to go home. She didn't want any trouble. Why did she deserve all this?

At that, Peggie felt queasy and fell on her side. Holding her broken nose, she reached for phone and called for help.

CHAPTER 4

Showtime

THE PARKING lot just outside of the Shadow Carnival's tent was full the following day. Crowds of people flowed into the tent, all rushing to find their seats, while others tried to see how many snacks they could carry to their seats. Children were throwing fits about wanting to go home, but others were excited.

Backstage, the freaks were running around, giddy with excitement. Freaks were lined up side by side, applying makeup in front of mirrors … as if they needed any more. Dodie was walking around, checking everyone and all the props, marking them off a checklist. Janette merely watched from atop a crate, smiling as things unfolded. Mimi was posing in front of a mirror and blowing kisses to herself.

"This is it," Mimi squealed to herself, listening to the din of the audience from within the tent. She reached for a feathery pink scarf and draped it over her shoulders.

"All of those people are here to see me," she said, chuckling. "It's only natural, after all—I'm what they really want: the star of the show."

"Mimi!" Dodie suddenly shrieked, startling everyone.

The freaks quickly got out of Dodie's path and watched with curiosity as she stormed over to her target. Mimi put on her best smile and her ridiculous sunglasses as she went into diva mode. "Yes?" she answered casually.

Dodie opened up a notebook and pushed it into Mimi's face. Act names were scrawled across time blocks.

"What's this?" Mimi asked with a giggle.

Dodie stamped her foot. "You know what it is. It's the schedule."

"What about it?" Mimi replied nonchalantly.

"You messed with it," Dodie said accusingly.

Mimi rolled her eyes and returned to the mirror to continue applying blush to her cheeks. "What makes you think it was me?"

"I don't know—maybe because your name is on all the time blocks, scheduled to sing during all of them?"

Mimi's jaw dropped with an exaggerated gasp, "Really? How thoughtful. It was the right choice. After all, I'm the reason there's an audience." She returned to the mirror to gussy herself up.

Dodie held her forehead as if it would fall off, sighing in aggravation. "You can't possibly believe that."

"Of course I do. Here's the evidence." Mimi tore off a flyer that was taped to the mirror and showed it to her. It was a picture showing a close-up of Janette's face with the tent in the background. Janette's portrait was surrounded by an oval with aesthetically pleasing borders and a ribbon at the bottom. "Shadow Carnival" was written on it. To the right of Janette was text containing information on showtimes and their address.

Dodie frowned. "What am I looking at?"

Mimi pointed to the bottom left corner of the flyer. A small picture of Mimi posing seductively on her back had secretly made its way into the flyer.

"See? Proof," Mimi bellowed in triumph.

"But people can barely see you," Dodie argued.

"Because it's subliminal advertisement. You wouldn't understand." Mimi brushed off her comment.

"What I don't understand is that you know what subliminal advertisement is. The schedule was made for a reason," Dodie lectured.

"Then follow the schedule! Now would you please be a dear and get my stage ready? It's what was planned, after all." Mimi began vocal exercises.

Dodie was furious. "I'll say it again: No one wants to listen to you."

Mimi ignored her and cleared her throat. "Do, re, mi, mi, mi ..."

Fuming, Dodie stormed off to go tattle to Janette, who was busy talking and being entertained by the freaks. As soon as Janette caught sight of Dodie, she sent the giggling band of troublemakers on their way.

"Hello, Dodie. You look like you're having fun." Janette smirked from atop the crates.

"Lazy as always, I see." Dodie spouted.

"I'm management. Doing nothing most of the time comes with the job."

"I have some work for you then." Dodie handed her the schedule.

"Did Mimi mess with it?" Janette asked.

"So you know?" Dodie was ready to blow another gasket.

"Please—the whole circus heard you. Now I know you like to make a big deal of things so it can't be that ba ... Oh!" Janette gawked at the schedule, but mostly she gawked at the introduction. Apparently Mimi had taken Janette's place as host of the show.

"I was willing to put up with her so long as she actually helped, but this out of hand." Dodie said angrily.

Janette glared at Mimi as she slid off the crates and onto the ground.

"I hope you're going to take care of this," Dodie threatened.

Janette returned the schedule and replied, "No need to worry. I'll take care of her. You do have a backup to the schedule right?"

"As a matter of fact, I do," Dodie chirped, showing off her dedication to the group.

"Good, we'll use that, but make a quick change." Janette exchanged a mischievous smirk with Dodie as showtime drew near.

Moments later, Mimi appeared in her blue, glitter-covered dress, looking like she was going to a high-class club. She gripped the microphone tightly as she watched the audience from behind the curtain of the back entrance. The din of the audience's conversations sounded through the tent. Lights from cameras flashed like stars.

"This is it," she thought to herself. "I'm actually going to sing in front of an audience. Oh my gosh, do I look okay? Do I have anything in my teeth? Did I even brush my teeth? Oh gosh!" She began to pace and fidget. She was both excited and nervous because this was her first audience that wasn't the Shadow Carnival.

"Mimi!" Janette called out, approaching from behind and startling Mimi. Janette pushed a gold-colored headset into her hand. She explained to confused Mimi: "I didn't think this would be ready on time, but Dodie managed to pull it off. This headset will pick up your voice better."

Mimi's face lit up and she examined the headset. She smiled and teared from this sudden display of kindness. "Thank you. I'm glad you understand."

"Understand?" Janette was puzzled.

"You're not like Dodie. I asked her before if I could sing. She didn't approve."

"Why not?"

Mimi bit her lip in frustration and said sternly: "She said no one wants to listen to me."

"I see. So that's why you tampered with the schedule."

"Are you mad?"

"I'll let it slide just this once. Now go out there and give them a show they won't forget!'"

With this bit of encouragement, and equipped with the headset, Mimi took a deep breath and journeyed to the center ring.

"Hello everyone," she bellowed into the microphone. The baffled audience stared at her. "First ... I'm going to sing." She posed like a diva. Giggles came from the audience. Mimi was concerned by this but paid no attention.

She cleared her throat and with all her heart began to sing a short song: "You don't know me, but you should know. I'm who you want to be," she began, singing some of the most self-absorbed lyrics ever known to humankind. The audience's laughter became a deafening din.

Mimi stopped and stared in disbelief. This wasn't like she'd hoped it would be.

"Come on, guys, let's save the laughter for later." Despite reasoning with them, the laughter continued. Mimi removed her headset. "What's so … funny?" Mimi heard a chipmunk version of her voice blaring over the speakers.

With her ears uncovered, the din of the audience was like a thunderstorm. It could even be heard outside the tent. Escaping from it was impossible. Mimi stared at the golden headset in disbelief as she raised the microphone to her mouth. "Hello?" she said quietly into it, and the same distorted voice was heard throughout the tent.

A shocked sense of embarrassment took over. Mimi's resolve to sing evaporated quickly as she turned away. Mimi's eyes watered as she scurried toward backstage and past Janette, who wore a big grin.

Dodie entered the tent looking content. "That'll teach her not to mess with the schedule," she said triumphantly.

"Not to mention the audience loved it," Janette replied, seeing the audience's beaming faces.

"Ah, two birds with one stone. And here I thought you were just lazy," Dodie said, impressed by Janette's cleverness.

Janette strolled into the ring, waving to the audience. "I sure hope you liked that first act. Here at the Shadow Carnival, it's all about having fun." There was a malicious look in her eye.

"I am Janette, your host. Now that the introductions are over, let's begin."

An array of special effects devices went off, sparklers spewed sparks into the air that rained down around the ring, and an oddly familiar smoke covered the area in a light layer of fog. Some coughs came from the audience. Some of them didn't feel quite like themselves.

CHAPTER 5

Questioning

A FTER BEING bedridden for a day, Peggie found herself sitting in the lobby of the local police station. Her cheek ached. A purple bruise showed where Sally Sock'em hit her. Her nose was held in place by a cast. Police officers entered and exited the entrance with newly apprehended criminals, some of whom were yelling that they wanted to see their lawyers as they were being taken in for questioning.

Peggie's mother, who had long black hair, olive skin, and brown almond eyes, sat next to her, attempting to comfort anxious Peggie.

"You're not in trouble. They just want to ask you what happened is all," her mother said in comfort while Peggie just looked at the floor.

What am I supposed to say? Peggie thought, questioning her own sanity.

Ms. Worth, Peggie's Mom, asked in desperation: "Can you at least tell me what happened?"

"I'm not too sure what happened," she replied.

A policeman came by and escorted Peggie to a small room with only a wooden table, two chairs, and blindingly bright lights, passing a fire extinguisher on the way. A tall bald man asked her to sit.

Peggie sat directly across from the one-way window of the type typically found in police dramas. Peggie didn't even have time to get settled before being bombarded with questions.

"So Peggie, what is your relationship with Sal?" the agent asked. His badge reflected light into Peggie's face so brightly she couldn't even tell what color his suit was.

"I … I … I don't know her … all that much." Peggie averted her eyes from the officer in order not to be blinded.

"Are you sure?" the officer seeing this asked.

"Y-yes … M-my eyes hurt. Um … I always thought you police people kept your badge things in your wallets." A bang came from the other side of the window. Apparently it was an I-told-you-so sign from a frustrated co-worker. Tucking his badge away, the agent cleared his throat and sheepishly continued the interrogation.

"So Peggie, what exactly happened the last time you saw Sal?" the agent asked.

Peggie had been staring at the table. She looked up hesitantly and replied, "She was trying to get money from me."

"She was trying to mug you?" the agent asked, and Peggie nodded firmly.

At that moment Peggie figured out what to say. "I … I told her that I didn't have any money on me. Sh-she didn't believe me at first, and then … she hit me … She hit me and then she left."

"Was she going through hard times?" the agent asked, reviving a memory within Peggie's mind. Peggie recalled Sal's emotional fit and what she had pieced together from Sal's bruise. After answering several more questions, the agent returned Peggie to her mother, who in turn began interrogating the agent herself.

"Is everything okay with her?" she asked.

The agent smiled reassuringly. "She's fine. We're just trying to figure out whether Sal ran away. Your daughter's story matches with some of the evidence we've collected. I'm sure we'll be able to track Sal down in no time."

Ms. Worth's face seemed doubtful. "So you don't think this has anything to do with the kidnappings?"

The agent briefly looked away before saying, "There's no need to worry. There hasn't been any evidence to support kidnapping of any kind. If you'll excuse me, I have to get back. You two be safe now."

There wouldn't be evidence of kidnapping. The evidence was Sal herself: she had been kidnapped. So after that terrible attempt at trying to cover the police's lack of progress, the agent left the two and returned to his duties.

Peggie glanced at the digital clock hanging on the wall, which read twelve fifteen. "Mom, I need to get to school. My extra credit is today," she said.

"I know, dear." The two exited through the class doors, down the stone steps, and headed around to the parking lot on the side, to a small silver car, and drove off to the school.

They arrived in the school parking lot, crafted from red weathered bricks. The emblem of the school mascot, the Wayton Rabbit, clung to the highest wall.

Peggie climbed out of the car, wondering what they were going to have her do. Her mother called from the car window: "When should I come pick you up?"

"I'll call," Peggie replied, tired from her visit to the police department.

"Are you sure you're feeling all right?" her mother asked, looking concerned. Peggie smiled reassuringly. "I'm fine."

"All right."

Peggie made her way to the glass double doors of the school. She navigated her way through the locker-lined halls and turned a corner to the entrance to the auditorium. The large stage sat at the bottom off the sea of red chairs. The stage was brightly lit as students from the drama class prepared the stage. Set pieces were still being painted, assembled, and moved onto the stage.

As Peggie climbed down the steps, a familiar voice called her name and waved. It was Zack. Standing next to him was a grumpy baldhead whose plaid shirt and tan overalls were hard to miss.

"Ah, there you are," the grumpy man said.

"So ... what do I need to do, Mr. Burgley?" Peggie asked, having no clue where to begin.

"The play is *Rapunzel*. You know what that is, right?" Mr. Burgley grumbled, looking down at her with low expectations.

"Y-yes," Peggie stuttered.

"Don't raise your voice. I don't need any troublemakers. You two go help with the background props. I want the castle finished by five."

Zack rolled his eyes. "Yes sir." Mr. Burgley was going to respond but instead exhaled loudly.

"When you're painting it, make it look old, but not *too* old. It has to look pristine, but not *too* pristine. The castle is part of an important scene, so it has to be perfect. Do I make myself clear?" Mr. Burgley snapped.

"Yes," the two replied listlessly before being sent on their way.

"What does *pristine* mean?" Peggie asked, confused.

"I dunno ... clean?" Zack guessed as they clambered up onto the stage. They strolled over to a red-headed, blue-eyed, freckle-faced girl, who had already begun painting the cardboard castle on the floor.

"Okay, so what color?" Peggie asked, reaching for a paint bucket.

"I'd say he probably wants it to be tinted gray. White should be the base color. That way it looks a little dirty." Zack suggested as he pictured the castle in his mind. Peggie's face was filled with terror.

"I don't know how to do that," Peggie said, gasping.

"Wouldn't be the first time," the red-headed girl rudely interjected.

"Oh, it's you," Zack muttered as the girl rose from the floor.

"I should be saying that," the girl fired back, crinkling her nose and giving him a dirty look.

"Hi, April," Peggie said.

April crossed her arms and glared at them, "So you two are here to help? That old fart must be delirious. The last thing we need is a useless know-it-all, and a no-talent artist."

"At least we only have to put up with you till May," Zack said, smirking.

"What are you talking about?" April asked, confused. Zack looked saw Peggie was at a loss, too.

"You're named after a month," Zack explained.

April smiled. "Ha, was that supposed to be an insult? At least I don't have dirt for hair." The conversation had dissolved into childish banter.

Peggie spoke up: "Can we start on the castle now?"

"Fine, whatever the princess wants." April rolled her eyes and went back to painting. Zack got onto the floor, and just when Peggie thought they were in the clear, it started again.

"What are you using blue for?" Zack asked critically.

"Uh ... to make it stand out," April said defensively.

"It's a castle. It already stands out," Zack argued.

"When is this going to be over?" Peggie asked.

Some time had passed because Peggie took a trip to the restroom. She ran her hands under the cold faucet water, rinsing the soap bubbles away; grabbed a paper towel from the dispenser; and thoroughly dried her hands.

"Excuse me," a voice called to her.

Peggie looked behind her but saw no one there. She figured it was just someone outside the restroom and headed toward the exit.

"I said excuse me," the voice bellowed.

Peggie turned around again, positive the voice came from behind her. "Is someone there?" she asked and walked toward the bathroom stalls.

Suddenly, the faucet turned on by itself. Unnerved, Peggie stared at the sink.

Then the faucet turned itself off and the voice said, "Now that I have your attention, can we talk?"

"Wh-who said that?" Peggie stuttered as she backed her way into a corner.

"It's me ... from the other day," the voice explained. Peggie gasped.

"You're ... Who are you? What did you do to me?" Peggie cried as her eyes darted around the room.

"My name is Jane, and I'm a ghost. As for what I did I ... I awakened your power."

Overwhelmed with confusion, Peggie questioned her sanity.

"Ghost? ... Power? ... What are you talking about?" Peggie asked.

"I'm talking about magic," the ghost explained. "Everyone has magic locked away inside. To help you, I used my power to unlock yours. It's the only way to stop freaks."

Peggie removed herself from the wall and cautiously entered the center of the room. "Freaks?"

"Yes. The Shadow Carnival, where that girl Janette came from, likes to kidnap people and *freakify* them. That girl Sal was freakified. If you hadn't fought, she wouldn't have changed back. Worse, you would have died."

Peggie stared at the floor as she recalled the event. "So she was turned into ... a freak?" she asked, unsure she heard right.

"Right. I've been trying to stop them, but ... I'm a ghost. I can't do much of anything."

Peggie stared at the mirror and pretended to talk to her reflection. "But why? Why do they want to do that? What does this have to do with me?"

"To be honest, I guess it doesn't have anything to do with you. I'm just looking for someone to help. As for why they're doing this ... I wish I knew. I thought that since you encountered them, and I gave you your power, maybe you could help. Do you want to help?"

Peggie couldn't help but be upset by this. "What? No! No, absolutely not," Peggie shrieked.

"But ..." Jane pleaded.

"No! I don't want anything to do with this." The words *Princess Do Nothing* popped into her mind. Peggie looked at the floor again, struck with guilt.

"I see. But ... if no one stops them, more people will get kidnapped. Even worse, they'll get freakified."

Peggie thought about the recent string of kidnappings occurring within town and guessed the Shadow Carnival was behind them. "Sorry, you're going to have to ask someone else. I just want to be left alone. Is that so much to ask?"

Jane fell silent as she took a minute to absorb this disheartening answer. "All right, I tried. I'm sorry, I won't bug you. I can ask someone else." Then she gasped as screaming echoed through the halls. "What was that?"

"What happened?" Peggie asked as if she would get an answer.

"We have to go see," Jane urged.

"Wait, shouldn't we just stay here?" There was no response.

"A-are you still here?" Peggie asked, but no one replied. She grimaced as she made her way toward the auditorium.

CHAPTER 6

Comedy Gold

PEGGIE CAUTIOUSLY entered the auditorium and was struck with shock at the sight before her. Everyone was tied down to the chairs, as if they were forced to be an audience. Onstage was a red-headed female wearing a ridiculous getup: a beat-up red top hat and coat. Her face was plastered with white face paint, and large red lips were painted on her to make her look like she was always smiling. A flower was in her coat pocket. Strapped to her waist was a miniature speaker attached to a microphone. Accompanying that speaker was … a rubber chicken?

"Hello, everyone, and welcome to Wayton High Comedy Night," the girl said into the microphone. "It's me, the loveable star … April Fool!" she said to introduce herself while giant neon letters spelling out APRIL descended from above. The letter *A* in this sign was faulty.

It broke off and crashed into the stage. Sparks momentarily gushed out as it shattered onstage.

In response, April hit a button on the audio device strapped to her waist, and the sound of an audience applauding and whistling echoed from it.

"April?" Peggie gasped in shock, seeing that another person she knew had become a freak.

"April, release us this instant!" Mr. Burgley ordered as he struggled to get free.

"I demand that you let us go this instant!" April mocked. She pushed a button on the audio device. The sound of an audience laughing was heard throughout the auditorium. April's face lit up. She was convinced she was actually being applauded.

"Well, Mr. Grumpy, I'll soon cure you of your unpleasant disposition. Let the comedy begin."

"You have to fight her," Jane insisted, which startled Peggie.

"What? No, I can't fight. I ... I don't want to."

Jane argued: "Peggie, you've got no choice right now. New freaks are highly unstable. Not even the Shadow Carnival can control them, so if you don't fight, she's going to hurt someone."

Peggie was struck by another wave of guilt.

April scanned the audience and became giddy over her first victim. "Hey, Sarah," she called.

"Wh-what is it April?" a frightened overweight girl replied.

"How was prison?"

"What?"

"You know—for all the property you destroyed just by walking down the street." April chuckled and pushed another button. The sound of a drum and more prerecorded laughter filled the room. She moved on to her next victim.

"Mr. Burgley."

"What is it?" he replied.

"I finally know why you aren't married."

Mr. Burgley looked around the room nervously. "You do?"

"It's so obvious now: Women don't even know you're there because they're blinded by that shiny skull." Again April played prerecorded sounds.

"I know—I'll call the police," Peggie said, fumbling for her cell.

"You can't wait for them," Jane insisted.

"She hasn't hurt anyone yet," Peggie argued, determined not to get involved.

"That's enough, April," Zack yelled. He walked onto the stage wielding a pipe. Peggie gasped as she saw him approach the freak.

"Zack, no! She's dangerous," Peggie called out to him.

"Pegs, get out of here," he ordered, briefly looking away from April. By the time he looked back at April, she had lassoed him with the microphone cord. "What the heck?" he cried in surprise.

"Don't try to one-up me," April yelled. She spun around, lifted him into the air, and swung him around. "This one's a doozy," she said, smirking and flinging him into the wall. Zack slammed into the wall with a loud thud and crashed through several stage props on his way to the floor. The collision with the side of his back left him reeling in pain.

"Zack!" Peggie screamed, terrified at the sight of her injured friend.

April frowned when she spotted Peggie. "Hey, don't you know you're supposed to be seated for this kind of thing?" Zack got up slowly because his back was searing with pain. He slowly raised the pipe as he approached.

"Jane!" Peggie pleaded to the air, but she didn't have to say anything. Jane had already knocked April to the floor and brought down red velvet curtains to hide the stage from view. Confused, Zack felt a force pull on his arm: it was Jane leading him away from April.

Peggie was relieved to see her friend led toward the side exit.

The frightened voice of Mr. Burgley filled the air: "Someone get me out of here!" Peggie rushed down the stairs to untie the ropes, muttering nervously to herself.

"Quick, help me get everyone," Peggie tried to say, but she was pushed aside.

"Forget that," Burgley shouted as he ran for safety.

"Mr. Burgley!" Peggie cried desperately. Just then she heard April stomp when she jumped out from behind the curtain.

"Hey, you're ruining my act. Get up here." April pouted and swung her microphone like a lasso.

Peggie screamed and tried to run, but the microphone looped around her. The cord squeezed her chest tightly and lifted her into the air. April swung Peggie into the curtain, cackling like a little kid. Peggie crashed and rolled across the floor, yelping with pain.

April went through the curtain and gave Peggie the biggest forced smile ever seen. April then skipped merrily toward her victim while Peggie was getting up. With a cloud of purple smoke, April conjured up a metal mallet.

"This stage isn't big enough for the both of us." April swung her mallet and bashed it against Peggie's skull. Peggie once again landed on the floor, hurting her arm as her scalp began to bleed. April reached for her rubber chicken.

"It's time to bring out the big guns," April proclaimed. She pointed the chicken at Peggie and pulled its head back. As the neck collapsed, the barrel of a shotgun ejected from the prop's beak, leaving Peggie horribly confused.

"It's *geek* hunting season. Get it? Get it, get it, get it? I said *geek* instead of *geese*, and this is a *chicken*," April babbled. She gripped the legs of the chicken, ready to pull. Peggie cringed, closed her eyes, and began to cry.

"April," Zack called. He climbed up the stairs to the stage.

April glared at him and growled, "Ugh! You again?" Zack held out his hand as if telling her to stop. April smirked as she pointed the gun at him.

A thunderous clap boomed as April was zapped by a bolt of lightning. She dropped the gun and fell on it, causing it to go off. Screams could be heard from the audience.

"Oh my god, he's been shot!" a girl cried. A boy grimaced in agony.

Zack's jaw dropped in horror at this accident. Peggie stared at the both of them, trying to figure out what happened. April got up, looked around, put a smile on her face, and said, "I guess that was the magic bullet." Again prerecorded comedy sounds played. Peggie was amazed by how indifferently April was behaving.

She wondered if this was what the Shadow Carnival was doing to people. April made her way toward the gun again.

"It's always funny the second time." April cheered as she picked up the gun.

Peggie held out her hand and screamed at her: "April stop it!" Another glassy orb of mist fired from her hand. It crashed into April's leg, knocking her to the floor in a cloud of mist. The gun then took to the air, taken away by Jane the ghost. The prerecorded laughter went off again, this time in endless loops. The device must've finally broken from all the roughhousing.

Hearing the laughter play over and over, April stood up, shaking with terror. She turned to the curtain as her eyes filled with TV static. "S-stop it. I-it's not funny," she demanded, yelling toward her captive audience.

The laughter continued as April broke into tears. "Stop laughing! There's ... there's nothing wrong with me. Stop it! I said stop it! *Stop laughing at me!*" she screamed at the top of her lungs, demanding silence.

Peggie and Zack stared at her, baffled by this change in behavior. "Peggie, Zack—she's flickering. Hit her now and this'll stop," Jane said to alert them while April's face was turning burning red.

"I'll give you something to laugh about," April screamed. A large box appeared in her hands. The doors on the front of this box opened up, and the barrel of a small cannon elongated toward the audience.

Peggie and Zack held out their hands and launched spells. April was consumed by a thick mist, screaming as she was zapped by lightning as if she was being eaten alive by a storm cloud. The cloud began to glow, becoming a ball of bright light.

"You guys can't take joke," April whined. Then the ball burst into a bright flash.

When police sirens filled the air, April fell to the floor and Peggie and Zack ran to her side.

"She looks normal again." Zack said, sighing with relief and falling to his knees, overcome by illness. His head hung low and his stomach churned. "I don't fell goo-*blargh!*" Zack emptied his stomach onto the floor and lay down on his back, ready to pass out.

"Zack? Zack!" Peggie cried, worried about her friend. The doors of the auditorium slammed against the walls. A thunderous tumult of footsteps came rushing down the stairs. Peggie's face lit up: Help had finally arrived.

She heard people shouting at each other. "Get this boy on a stretcher!"

"Over here on the stage—we need help," Peggie said. Two officers rushed up the stairs and over to their side.

"Are you all right? What happened here?" one of the officers asked while they prepared to whisk Zack and April away. But Peggie just stared at the floor. It never occurred to her that she'd be questioned again.

"It's ... hard to say. I just want to get out of here first. That's more important right now, isn't it? You can question me later. Just help them," she said with genuine urgency.

This worked; the officers whisked the two away. Peggie followed them down the stairs. Glancing around the auditorium, she saw captive students being led out by the police. One student was being carried out on a stretcher through the side door. She glanced back at the seats where the students had been held prisoner. One seat was stained with blood, and puddles had formed on the floor. The scene burned into her mind as something she would never forget.

Peggie thought, *This was the Shadow Carnival's doing. If I hadn't done something, it could've been a lot worse*, as she was led out the door. The unforgettable event continued when she and all the students were taken to the hospital for examination and care.

CHAPTER 7

Flying Solo

A FEW WEEKS later, back at the Shadow Carnival, Mimi was in her personal dressing room. It was like a small apartment that was cluttered with makeup, clothes racks, mirrors, diet pills, glamour magazines, and studio lights.

Mimi was sitting in front of a mirror with bottles of makeup, cluttering the desk before her. She was wearing protective goggles and a lab coat strategically buttoned to show cleavage. She was pouring multicolored powders into bottles filled with putrid-smelling liquids.

A puff of purple smoke exploded from the bottles, polluting the air, making Mimi choke and gag on the nauseas fumes. She waved the smoke away with her hands before examining her creation. As she stared intently at the bottles, a great big smile spread across her face.

"Aha!" she cried. She took one bottle and kissed the glass, then reached for a plastic Darcy Doll and an eye dropper. She filled the dropper with the makeup, gripped the doll tightly in her hand, squeezed one drop of her makeup onto the doll's face, and watched it melt away as it steamed. The smell of burnt plastic filled the air as Mimi got up and danced around excitedly.

"Yes—With this I'll be the only one worth looking at." She giggled and kissed the glass bottle, leaving lipstick behind. She sampled some of this new lotion she made for herself, rubbing it into her skin with no noticeable repercussions.

When she tired of admiring herself, she packed her things into several large suitcases, exited her trailer, and headed across the lot. Many of the freaks roaming about pointed and giggled at her. This irked Mimi, but she didn't care because she was moving on to bigger and better things—until Dodie caught her.

"Mimi!" Dodie's shrill voice rang as she ran to catch up with Mimi, who looked back at her wearing her ridiculous sunglasses.

"Yeah?"

"Don't 'yeah' me," Dodie glared. "You've haven't been participating in the shows. I demand that you start rehearsing for Saturday." Dodie glared at Mimi, who just looked away.

"I've rehearsed for a different gig," she said. Dodie was bewildered by this statement but then noticed Mimi carrying luggage.

"Are you leaving just because of some faulty equipment? Can you be even more of a child?"

"Faulty? Ha! I know it was you who sabotaged me. I can't work in these conditions. You're just holding me back because you're jealous."

Dodie's face turned red. "Me, jealous? Of all the stupid things I've heard ..."

"Going at it again and you didn't tell me?" Janette interrupted.

Dodie smiled as she tattled. "Mimi here is leaving." Janette stopped in her tracks, shocked to hear this news.

"I'm sure you're just exaggerating," Janette said, playing it off and putting on a smile.

Mimi looked at Janette apologetically. "No—I *am* leaving." The color drained from Janette's face.

"But you can't," Janette insisted.

"I can, and I will. I'm going to be a star, and I can't do that here."

Janette was dumbfounded. Dodie noticed this and shook her head with disappointment.

"We'll be better off without you anyway," Dodie jibed.

"Same here. Oh boys," Mimi called, and two freaks dressed like bouncers ran to her side. Both of them had numbers on their shirts. The African American male was adorned with *1* while the Caucasian male was given *2*.

"Hold these for me," Mimi ordered, passing them the suitcases that nearly tore their arms off from the weight.

"You're taking these boys with you?" Dodie asked. Mimi scoffed.

"Of course I am. Every star needs an entourage. Come along now," Mimi called and led the way into the parking lot.

"Yes … Mimi," the freaks replied worshipfully and wobbled along behind her.

"What's taking you guys so long?"

"Sorry … Mimi."

"Don't worry. Once you get a taste of Burn, it won't be a problem anymore." Janette and Dodie stared as the group took off.

She actually left me, Janette thought with her mouth agape.

Dodie smiled and felt light on her feet. "Now that that bug's out of the way, we can move on to more important things." She waited for a reply, but Janette was still shocked.

"Janette?" Dodie asked, tapping on her shoulder.

"Yes?" Janette said, coming back to reality.

"We have an issue that needs taking care of." Dodie led the way into the tent. A large group of freaks were gathered around, whispering in hushed voices as if discussing plays during a football game.

"What's the problem, Dodie?" Janette asked. Dodie pointed to the group of freaks, who moved out of the way, revealing an empty chair.

"I don't get it," Janette said, puzzled.

Dodie glanced at the chair and went into a rampage. "Where is he?"

"Uh … who?" one of the freaks asked nervously.

"Paranoid! Paranoid Paul, the lunatic. Where is he?" Dodie screamed, getting in their face with her nostrils flaring.

"Oh, him. Uh ... I don't know?" The freak hesitantly replied. At that moment a large dictionary appeared in Dodie's hand, and she smacked him in the face with it. The freak fell to the floor, and all the others gasped and backed away in fear.

"Well, find him!" Dodie demanded, and they all scurried off to search for the lunatic.

"I take it we have a lunatic?" Janette asked, smirking while Dodie tried to calm down.

Dodie huffed and said: "Yes, and he's not the only one we collected recently. We have a few more that are getting out of hand." Janette was about to reply when they heard a man shrieking.

"Ah! They found me! They're here! Run!" the voice cried, and the freaks chased him.

"Paranoid, stop it, we just want to lock you up," one of the freaks bellowed.

"I take it that's Paul?" Janette asked.

Dodie nodded. "Unfortunately, yes."

"What's so bad about ..."

"They've touched me! I've been infected! It burns!" Paranoid Paul screamed.

"It doesn't sound that ..." Janette tried to say before getting cut off.

"Oh no! I feel myself changing! No! Your disease will not take me!" Paranoid Paul shouted. Soon after, the air reverberated with the sound of a gunshot, rendering Dodie and Janette silent for a moment.

Dodie cleared her throat. "Well ... that problem took care of itself."

"So we're done?" Janette asked.

Dodie shook her head, "No, not in the slightest. Come with me."

She led Janette to the back of the tent, where they kept props for the show. More freaks were gathered around a very loud female. This freak wore a teddy bear beanie, a small, pink tank top with a heart, and tight shorts. Her most noticeable feature was that she wore one glove that resembled a bear's paw.

"Do you like me?" the girl desperately asked a male freak she'd grabbed by the shirt.

"Uh ... I ... I ..." The male freak stuttered.

"I said, 'Do you like me?'" she shouted, shaking him violently.

"You're all dismissed," Dodie announced, and the freaks fled as if there were a fire.

"Oh, she's a teddy bear. How cute. So what's wrong with this one?"

"This is Amanda Bear. Give her a second." Amanda approached with probing eyes. She stood over Janette with an intimidating posture and glared at her. Janette waited patiently, anxious to see what the fuss was about.

Amanda took a deep breath. "Do you like me?"

Janette glanced at Dodie, who gestured to go ahead.

"Sure," Janette replied."

"Are you sure?"

"Yes."

"Really?" Janette looked at Dodie, who gestured once again.

"Yes?" Janette answered wearily.

"Really?"

"Yes?" Janette slowly answered again.

"Really?"

Janette thought this was odd, so this time she answered no. Amanda's face fumed a bright red color.

"I knew it. Why don't you like me? Like me *right now!*" Amanda screamed. Blades emerged from her glove like a claw. She shrieked with rage and swung at Janette, but she stepped aside and tripped Amanda, who did a face plant into the dirt. Amanda stood up and shook with rage. She charged at the nearest chair. Wielding it, she went around the room and started smashing all the props.

"Like me! Like me! Like me!" Amanda demanded like a child throwing a tantrum.

Dodie commented: "Attention-needy brats are the second most hated on my list, not far behind children. So Janette how about you? How does this rank on your list?"

Amanda tossed the chair aside, lay down on the floor, and screamed and kicked and yelled, pounding her fists on the ground.

"Okay, Dodie, I see your point. We have to put them somewhere."

Janette removed her hat and traced her finger along the brim. Amanda's feet left the ground, and she hovered in the air.

"Put me down and like me!" she demanded before getting sucked into the hat.

"No! No! I didn't mean it!" she screamed as the hat ate her.

"There, that'll do," Janette said with a smirk.

"There are a few more to deal with." Dodie said.

Janette moaned reluctantly. "All right, Dodie I'll take care of it." With that, Janette tried to leave.

However, Dodie posed a question. "Janette, while we're on this subject, I think it's time you told me. Why are you collecting so many freaks? Just what is it you plan to do?"

Janette replied nonchalantly: "Stuff."

CHAPTER 8

Coming to a Theater Near You

M S. WORTH came to answer a knock at the door. "Coming!" she bellowed as she ran up to the door and peeked through the eyehole and saw a brown-haired man at the door. Ms. Worth asked from behind the door, "Who is it?"

"It's me. Please, you have to let me talk to your daughter. She has to know where my Sal is. Please!" the man said, his voice quivering.

Ms. Worth's face became contorted. "Mr. Base, she already said all she knew to the police. This is the fourth time you've come here. Leave now or I will call the police."

Furious, Mr. Base desperately pounded his fist on the wall and continued to plea. Peggie was watching from the living room couch, pained with guilt and afraid of Sal's father. She stared at her reflection in the TV and recalled that Sal mentioned being hurt by her father. Peggie wondered if that meant she'd been abused. Meanwhile, Mr. Base's pleading devolved into threats and furious pounding on the door.

"That's it, I'm calling the police." Ms. Worth got out her cell and pressed speed dial. She had the volume on max and the speaker turned on to make sure that Mr. Base could hear.

"All right, all right, I'm going … bitch," he mumbled. He reluctantly made his way down the stairs of the apartment. Ms. Worth reported the incident to the police and planned to get a restraining order.

Peggie got off the couch and went to the window where she saw Mr. Base slamming his fist against a beat-up silver car. He hopped into the driver's seat and reached for what looked like a can of beer. He started to gulp it down, but he stopped halfway as if it overridden with guilt. He tossed the beer can out the window, its contents pooling into the street as he drove off. Her mother came over to her side and gently placed her hand on Peggie's shoulder.

"It's all right," she reassured as Peggie looked up at her with a worried look. Ms. Worth looked at the clock hanging above the TV and asked, "Do you really want to go out today?"

"Yeah, I made plans with Zack. He's already on his way there. I can't just leave him alone." Peggie had to convince her mother it was okay to go because she and Zack had decided to meet with Jane this day.

In the back of her mind, Peggie was thinking: "We need to figure out what we're going to do about the Shadow Carnival. Who are they? Where did they come from? How do I keep them away from me?" Meanwhile, she continued to reassure her mother.

Ms. Worth looked out the window. "I just don't want you getting into another incident. With the kidnapping and the shooting at school, it's getting dangerous out there."

"I know. That's why I'm going to the movies with Zack. We'll stay together. We'll also be in a place with a lot of people. It's safer when you're in a crowd. That's all the stuff you told me, isn't it?" Ms. Worth held her forehead, defeated.

"All right, just be careful."

"Things aren't that bad. I just … got unlucky. It can't happen a third time." That said, her mother gave her a suffocating hug.

"I love you. You know that, right?"

"Yes, Mom, I love you too." The pain of guilt stabbed at her heart.

"If anything happens again, you'll stay home for a bit, understood?"

"Yes, Mom."

With that, Peggie was dropped off at the theater. She said farewell to her mother before making her way toward the overglorified building. A neon sign that read "Wayton Views" hung over a large arch. Peggie passed through this mysterious gate and strolled down a red-tiled path leading to the ticket booth.

The word "Tickets" hung in bold white letters over the booth. The only thing needed to complete the entrance was large, flashing arrows. How else did they expect customers to find their way?

"Where are they? Am I early?" Peggie pondered as she viewed the wall that was plastered with movie posters.

"Peggie!" Jane shouted, scaring Peggie half to death.

"J-Jane! D-don't do that!" Peggie shouted, drawing attention. She sheepishly looked at the crowd and nervously retreated from view.

"Sorry. Anyway, I'm here. Where's Zack?"

Peggie looked around one more time and spotted Zack approaching from the parking lot.

"Hey, Zack," Peggie said with a friendly smile.

"Hey, Pegs. Is she here yet?" Zack looked around as if he could see her.

"I'm here," Jane announced, and both of them jumped.

"I'll never get used to this," Peggie said.

"I know. Isn't it, cool?" Zack enthusiastically replied.

"Glad to see someone who's happy to not see me," Jane said, chuckling. Zack put his fascination aside and took on a serious tone.

"So … before we watch a film, I have to ask, what exactly is going on? I mean what happened to April? If I hadn't called for help, Brad wouldn't have made it."

Peggie spoke up and shared what she knew: "From what I understand …" This left Zack with a curious look on his face.

"The Shadow Carnival? Really? We actually have an evil circus troupe in our city?" Zack asked skeptically.

Peggie nodded. "Yeah it seems that way." Peggie thought maybe he didn't believe her as he took a moment for this to sink in.

"So what do we do?" he asked eagerly.

Jane was astounded. "You're really into this, aren't you?"

"It's more exciting than math, that's for sure. Anyway, you know I don't like it when people go around acting like jerks. If there's something I can do, I'd rather do it, you know?"

"You're actually going to go along with this?" Peggie asked, puzzled by this reaction.

"Aren't you?" Zack replied, raising an eyebrow.

"No. I'm trying really hard not to get involved in this stuff. It's dangerous."

"That's surprising given how well you did. I'm sure if that sorry excuse of a person didn't leave us to die, everyone would have gotten out all right. I'm also sure that if the Shadow Carnival is anything like April, we'll be able to handle them without too much trouble."

Hearing this foolishly optimistic attitude, Jane spoke up. "Zack, that was because April's transformation was fresh. She was unstable. Freaks like that are the easiest to undo."

"How so?"

"The kind of magic the carnival uses is … incomplete," Jane answered nervously.

"Incomplete? What the heck does that mean?"

Jane spoke slowly, choosing her words with caution. "It's unstable. I don't know why it's unstable, but normally you would have to use a counter spell to undo something of that nature. With the Shadow Carnival, though, exposure to another source of magic erodes the spell. So the more you hit a freak with your powers, the weaker the spell gets until it breaks. So I guess you can say that the spell used on them isn't locked."

For clarification Peggie asked: "So we're just using brute force then?"

Jane nodded her invisible head. "Yeah, pretty much. So you guys are going to have to get better with using your powers. The freaks who aren't fresh will be fully under the carnival's control. They won't flicker or get distracted as easily, so you'll need to be more careful if you encounter them. Then you have the carnies to worry about if they ever make an appearance."

"Carnies?" Peggie repeated to the air, guessing were Jane was.

"Carnies are the people who basically work for and run the carnival. Janette is one of three and is the ringleader of the group. She has been responsible for the kidnappings and the freakification of her victims."

Peggie thought back to her first encounter with the carnival. "So Janette is the one behind all this."

"Really? Because April got freakified out of nowhere, and I didn't see a 'Janette' anywhere," Zack said, puzzling over this conundrum.

"Are you sure? Tell us everything that happened," Jane asked, perplexed.

Zack crossed his arms as he thought back to April's transformation. "We were working on the castle. Peggie left to go to the restroom. April was being a jerk as always, and ... then she got a really bad cough, and ... then a purple cloud ate her. The next thing I knew, I was on the floor, and April started going crazy. Everyone who was getting a sandwich from Burgley was caught by some spell. I called for help, and not too long after that you guys came."

"You didn't see anyone strange? I think she wears a top hat and looks like a magician." Peggie said, describing Janette.

"No, I think I would've noticed something as crazy as a magician girl in a top hat."

Jane muttered, "But that can't be right. All of the transformations were done in person before."

Zack asked, "Are you saying she changed her method?"

"Oh, God!" Jane exclaimed. "If she did, things are going to get bad unless we get rid of her. More incidents like what happened to April will occur, and anyone unlucky enough to be nearby ..." She trailed off, envisioning a gruesome scene of someone turning into a freak during an event like a wedding.

Peggie said, "If I see anyone acting weird, I'll just assume it's the carnival and run the other way."

"I guess I helped at least one person by spreading this information," Jane said.

Zack asked Peggie: "But if anyone could get freakified at any moment, where would you run to that would actually be safe?" attempting to motivate her to do something.

"Better than standing there like an idiot." She spoke from experience, recalling the rightly deserved punch she got from Sally Sock'em.

Zack continued to press the issue. "Something needs to be done about the carnival, Peggie."

She retaliated by snapping at him. "Then go do something about it! I don't want to have anything to do with this, and even if I did, I'm not cut out for this kind of stuff. So can we just watch a movie now? I want to get my mind off of this nonsense."

"Yeah, okay, I hear you; might as well. Since we're here, it'd be a shame to not watch anything." Zack's eyes wandered to the movie posters advertising both future and current films.

"Okay. So what are we going to watch?" Peggie looked over the choices that were prominently displayed above the ticket booth.

Jane spoke up. "I can give some recommendations since I've seen all of these movies already."

"Already?" Zack said. "Wow, that must've been expensive."

"Not if you're dead," Jane bragged in a singsong voice.

"Oh, right. So what's good to watch, then?" Zack asked, embarrassed that he forgot he was talking to a ghost.

Jane held her invisible chin and thought about it. "Most of these are your basic generic romance comedies and dramas, and those would be the most interesting ones. *Vengeance* is about superheroes, and the other one is *Bow Before the Mayor*."

"What's that mayor one about?" Peggie asked, intrigued by this title.

"Government oppression. A bit heavy with political talk, though," Jane said.

Zack objected: "I can't even memorize the Bill of Rights. If it's all political talk, I won't be able to understand half of it." He cast his vote for the superhero flick.

"That one was more fun to watch, and I'm still trying to decipher some of the jargon they used in the mayor movie. So I would recommend superheroes over anything," Jane said.

Peggie was afraid this movie would remind her of the carnival. "I guess we're watching that one, then."

"Aw, come on, don't be like that." Jane began to tell her experience excitedly, going over her favorite scenes. "Jordan Star is in this movie. I really liked his performance in *Never Let You Go*. His delivery of lines is so natural, and I even wanted to cry for the bad boy character he played. His character is really fun in this one, though. There's this one part where they're like in Russia and there's this snow witch …"

Zack cut her off. "Jane! Spoilers! Let all the good parts be a surprise for us, okay?"

Jane was embarrassed. "Sorry. I really liked that movie, and I can't wait to watch it again with you all. And Jordan is like my favorite actor. He is like so gorgeous now." She swooned at the thought of seeing him on screen again.

"You like the movie because of this one actor?" Zack asked.

"The whole movie is good, but I like movies like this. The men normally need to hit the gym for these roles. It isn't just him who looks good. Some of the other actors look much better."

"Gee, imagine the horror if these characters weren't muscle men," Zack sarcastically replied.

"Right. C'mon, let's get some tickets," Jane agreed.

They bought their tickets and entered through the glass doors, passing a fire extinguisher that was accompanied by a poster with fire safety regulations written on it.

"Hey!" Peggie cried when suddenly Mimi, wearing a trench coat and ludicrously large glasses, bumped into her. She was accompanied by two men who must've been body builders, judging by their massive size. Mimi didn't even look back but continued on, cleared her throat, and did some vocal exercises.

"People these days …" Zack muttered.

The large room was well lit. Many sat in the red seats, eagerly waiting for the film to start. The three of them marched up the steps and found seats in the middle next to April.

She was on the phone. "No, I'm not telling you where I am … I'll go home later … I don't need meds … There's nothing wrong with me … Ugh! Goodbye!" When she hung up, she noticed her neighbors.

"Ugh! Really?" she moaned.

"Oh, hi April," Peggie said, greeting her nervously.

"April's here?" Zack asked as he looked over Peggie. "Oh, brilliant," he mumbled.

April scowled. "Just don't bother me and we'll get along fine."

Peggie and Zack exchanged glances.

"So I guess she was released." Peggie said in a hushed tone.

"It figures that no one would believe she was turned into a freak," Zack replied. April looked away while catching bits and pieces of the conversation.

"All of the evidence vanished when she changed back, so it's not surprising she can't be convicted," Jane said.

"It's not her fault all that happened. She became a freak after all," Peggie replied. April gritted her teeth and her face turned red.

"Still, I don't want to sit next to her," Zack grumbled. Suddenly April rose from her seat and rushed out of the theater as if something were on fire.

"Y-you don't think she heard us, do you?" Peggie said, feeling somewhat ashamed.

"If she did, why does it matter?" Zack replied. The two fell silent once more. And April didn't return.

"So … how did it go—the voice actor job I mean?" Peggie asked, desperate to break the awkward silence.

"It … it was something." Zack said nervously, recalling his one-time performance.

"Oh, you a voiced a character?" Jane asked.

"Well, yeah. I was only like a side character with one line. 'They went that way' was all I said."

"What was it like, though? What did you do?" Peggie asked, trying to keep the conversation rolling. Zack thought back to standing in front of a microphone with people watching and listening.

"I had to do it a few times because they wanted the character to sound a certain way. So I had to talk in this squeaky voice … kind of embarrassing, really."

"I still think it's cool. Not many people get to have their voice recorded for stuff like that," Jane replied enviously.

"I would never be able to do something like that," Peggie added.

Zack smirked as he had a neat idea. "Maybe we can do it together next time."

"Oh, I … I don't know about that. Y-you know I-I think I'm good, so you don't have to do that." Peggie said sheepishly.

"I'll go," Jane said, volunteering.

"Jane, you're a ghost. How would that even work?" Zack reminded her.

But then the lights went out, and everyone's attention returned to the big screen that towered over them.

"Oh, it's starting," Jane said enthusiastically when commercials started playing. The first one was an advertisement for a cartoon that played on TV.

Zack's mouth dropped as he recognized the cartoon as the one he had voiced for. A clip of *Rufus the Rascal*, a children's cartoon, featuring a dog that gets into mischief, was displayed on screen. He noticed some of the annoyed and negative reactions of the people in the theater.

"They'll put anything on TV these days," a woman from above said to her husband. "Have you ever seen that show?" a boy from the row below asked his friend.

"Don't watch it, it sucks." His friend swiftly replied.

Zack felt himself shrinking when he heard the show he did voice work for being verbally bashed. To his relief, the advertisement changed to a commercial featuring beauty care products.

"Ladies, tired of being dumped? Tired of not being your best? Then try Burn!" Mimi enthusiastically presented this product while wearing racing attire, sprawled out across a red sports car at a race track. She was wearing a white jumpsuit that was not zipped all the way, just enough to make you wonder if she was wearing a bra.

Mimi got off the car and continued speaking as she walked over to a pair of muscular male underwear models with pectorals that stuck out an inch from their ribs and biceps so huge their own hands could not wrap around all the muscle.

"With Burn you'll leave all the other girls in the dust. Scientifically proven to enhance natural beauty by thirty percent. As for you guys out there: Trying to get in shape? Trying to get that muscular bod that'll make all the girls swoon? Then try Burntrition. It's an all-natural protein bar, clinically proven to increase muscle mass within two weeks of constant consumption. Remember: Looks don't matter, as long as you look good. And you can look good with Burn." Mimi wore a plastic smile that showed a mouth full of unrealistically white teeth.

Zack stared at the muscular men and then examined his own arms, which were twigs compared to the men. And his pectorals were not noticeable at all underneath his shirt. To their relief, the screen switched to another commercial.

"I wonder how many commercials are left?" Peggie wondered.

"There shouldn't be many," Zack said. Jane remained silent.

That was Mimi. What is she up to? Jane thought to herself, puzzled by the commercial.

When the third commercial came on, it was a repeat of the second commercial, and the audience groaned.

Zack grimaced. *Not this again,* he thought.

The ad replayed, but strangely, instead of stopping at the usual part, it continued on.

"And you can look good with Burn. Don't go just yet, though," Mimi said as if she were talking directly to the audience.

Mimi giggled. "Don't think I didn't notice that you were all bored before I appeared on the screen, right? Since you like me so much, I'll give you a real show to look forward to. I have to give the fans what they want, after all." The audience became confused. It seemed like the ad was talking to them.

This part didn't play last time, Peggie thought. Jane quickly caught on to what was happening.

"You guys need to get out of here now," Jane warned. The two of them noticed a faint white blur in the seat to their left.

"J-Jane, is that you?" Peggie asked.

Jane gasped. "Wait—You can see me now?"

"Only a little bit," Peggie replied.

The girl on the screen smiled. "There's something I've always wanted to do. Since I have an audience, let me introduce myself." With that Mimi sprinted toward the camera, coming closer and closer until finally a hole was punched in the screen and it burst wide open. Three people soared out of it with a cloud of confetti and smoke. The audience screamed with shock as Mimi, accompanied by two muscular bouncers, rose from the floor.

Gripping a microphone tightly, Mimi winked at the audience.

"Hello, everyone, it's so nice to see you. I'm the glorious, the beautiful, the talented Mimi," she announced. She was covered in smoke, and she had changed her costume to her standard rabbit outfit.

"And now for your feature presentation, I'll hold a private concert—just for you," Mimi announced and then blew a kiss to the audience.

Peggie and Zack exchanged glances in disbelief. The entire audience was speechless. "No! Not again!" Peggie whined and immediately thought of running away.

"I-is she a freak, too?" Zack asked, stunned.

"No, worse than that. She's Mimi, one of the carnies that run the carnival," Jane replied frantically.

The muscular clown-face-painted bouncers knelt beside Mimi like in a choreographed dance. Mimi began to do a jig and sing:

Don't you know that I'm hotter than the summer sun?

Say you love me! Hey, hey!

Don't you know I'm cooler than the winter breeze?

Say you love me!

"Shut up!" several people in the audience cried.

Mimi stumbled in mid-dance as she was taken aback by this.

"What kind of joke is this? This isn't what I paid for," another voice hollered. Mimi's jaw dropped when people started to get up and leave.

"Where's the manager? I want a refund," one woman yelled scornfully into the air.

What did I do wrong? I'm beautiful and I have talent. What more do they want? Mimi thought, her face contorted with disdain. Seeing the vexed audience make their way to the exit, Mimi stamped her foot. On command the doors swung closed, knocking people onto the floor.

There were cries from the startled audience. When they tried a second time to leave, they realized the doors were somehow sealed shut as if a magnetic force was keeping them closed. Sounds of panic and confusion rose from the audience. Mimi glared at the audience, fuming with rage. She turned the dial on her microphone and yelled into it.

"*Quiet!*" Her voice boomed through the speakers, followed by an earsplitting screech to get everyone's attention. Everyone stared at the psychopathic pop star as she continued.

"I came all the way here to sing. You all should be honored; you all should be cheering for me. So I'm … going … to … sing. And you're … going … to … like it." She screeched into the microphone, ordering her bouncers to escort everyone to their seats.

A few brave members of the audience lashed out against the bouncers but were swiftly knocked into the wall with the sound of snapping bones and painful murmurs.

Zack mentally prepared himself. "Let's get her!"

"No!" Jane objected, pulling him back into his seat.

"What? Why?" he asked, confused.

"There's too many people," Jane pointed out while everyone obediently returned to their seats. Peggie looked around nervously. The bouncers returned to Mimi's side, glaring intimidatingly at the audience.

"S-so what do we do?" Peggie asked.

Jane took a moment to think. "We're going to need help. We need to get everyone out … especially with Mimi here."

"Who's going to help us?" Zack asked.

"Quiet! This time I want no interruptions. You will all be cheering my name, I promise you. Just let me sing, and I'll show you how great I am," Mimi shouted frantically.

"I'll go find someone to help," Jane said. "You guys stay here. And don't do anything to make her mad."

"What happens if we do?" Zack whispered when Mimi began her song once more.

"She'll rip your head off," Jane replied emphatically. Then her shimmering body took to the air and faded through the wall.

CHAPTER 9

Now Playing

APRIL CAME out of the bathroom stall with a tear-stained face. She walked across the tiled bathroom floor and began washing her hands under the automated faucet.

"It happened again," she mumbled to herself, scrubbing her hands vigorously.

After drying her hands with a paper towel, she stared at herself in the mirror. She hung her head low over the sink.

"What did I do? What did I do that was so bad?" she asked herself, thinking back to the incident. She remembered waking up in a hospital bed and being terrified and confused, thinking that perhaps she was in a coma or that something else was wrong with her health. She remembered how the police came to her and questioned her, saying she was accused of shooting someone. She told them over and over, right up until she was finally discharged from the hospital, that she had no idea what had happened.

Naturally she had been temporarily suspended from school to give time for the commotion at the school to settle down and for things to get sorted out. But given how strange and absurd the claims were, the little information that was given was disregarded by all who investigated the matter. With no viable evidence to convict a guilty party, this left the whole affair in a shroud of uncertainty.

April finally pulled herself together and made her way toward the exit. Suddenly Jane's voice cried out: "April!"

April jumped. "Who's there? Were you listening?" she said in reaction, immediately putting on a tough-girl act.

"You can't see me, but you can hear me," Jane said.

"What do you mean I can't see you? Come out!" April demanded, approaching the stalls. One by one she opened the stalls but found no one in them.

The voice said, "My name is Jane, and I'm a ghost. I know you don't believe me."

"I don't believe you. Where are you?" April demanded, investigating every nook and cranny.

"April, look—I'll turn on the faucet," Jane said and then did it. April stared at the running faucet in bewilderment. "Remote controlled," she concluded.

"No, it's not. Why would anyone even do that?" Jane countered.

April fell silent for a moment, "I don't know. Because you're weird?"

"April, we don't have time for this. I need you to go back and open the doors to the theater."

"You mean like the entrance?" April investigated the ceiling above her.

"No! I mean where Peggie and Zack are. The doors are stuck, and no one can get out." April raised her eyebrow and continued to pointlessly scan the room.

"No. I'm not stupid. I know a prank when I see it," April said, scoffing and heading toward the door. Just then something pulled on her shirt, pulling her to the floor and dragging her across the room. She screamed as Jane took her for a ride.

"Let me go! Let me go!"

"If you would just listen for a second ... Ah!" Jane shouted in surprise when April unknowingly launched a fireball from her hand that burst across the tile of the bathroom wall.

Jane was briefly distracted by this sudden display of magical ability. April again made a mad dash for the door, which Jane thwarted by catching her again.

"April, wait! Calm down!"

"Someone help!"

"Shut up and I'll tell you what happened at school."

April looked up at her imaginary captor. "Y-you were there?"

"Yes, and that's why I need your help." Jane had regained her composure.

April rose from the floor and stared at the space she believed the ghost was in.

"Tell me first and I'll think about it," she replied sternly.

"All right, if that's the only way. Come look into the mirror, and I'll show you what happened."

April marched over to the mirror and stared at her reflection intently. It rippled and disappeared when it was replaced by a new image. The scene when April helped Mr. Burgley started to play on the mirror like on a TV. Her jaw dropped as she stared in amazement at this spectacle. She saw herself working on the castle with Zack, and she heard Peggie announce her trip to the bathroom.

"At least now there's only one of you," the April in the mirror commented snidely.

"Can't say the same for you," Zack snapped while he continued painting the castle.

April glared at Zack and dipped her brush in red paint and painted a few strokes on Zack's side.

"What the hell was that for?" Zack said.

"Oh, as if you didn't deserve it."

"Deserve what? You're the one who's making all the comments."

"Oh, and you haven't? 'Dirt for hair?'" she said.

Mr. Burgley announced that he had sandwiches for everyone and called the students to eat. They gathered around the box of food, but Zack and April continued arguing. April rose from the floor and continued her verbal bashing.

"You think you're so much better than everyone, but in reality you're not anything special. I happen to think that red looks better than your crappy painting." She smirked while trying to deal a low blow, coughing at the same time.

"Gosh, what is wrong with you? You must be some kind of freak to be this fricking hateful." Zack rose from the floor to get on her level.

"Freak? Me? I don't spend my time drawing cartoons for babies and children. How old are you again?" April continued to antagonize Zack but once again had to clear her throat. One of the students prompted the teacher to step in, but he merely shrugged it off and continued about his own business as the two continued their childish bickering.

"Mr. Burgley, she ruined the painting," Zack said, pointed at April's face.

"Then fix it," Mr. Burgley replied.

"Ha! Can't do anything without …" April coughed.

"Without …" She coughed again and continued to cough as her sudden illness escalated to the point she couldn't talk.

"I hope that's pneumonia I hear," Zack muttered hatefully. His attitude changed while April hacked up a storm until she found it difficult to breathe. She fell to her knees and continued coughing.

"Uhh … Hey, are you all right?" Zack asked. He got down to her level and noticed puffs of purple smoke were coming out of her mouth with each cough. Every time she coughed, the cloud got bigger. Zack backed away, and the teacher finally took interest in the situation.

"Hey, is she … okay?" Mr. Burgley's voice trailed off when April vanished behind the cloud and her coughing stopped.

Her whimpers of pain escalated into screaming. Flashes of light and thunder emanated from the cloud. A silhouette of April writhing in pain was visible through the cloud.

The cries of pain died down as the smoke vanished … leaving a freakified April standing before the class where she began to magically tie them down with restraints she conjured up and started babbling about some comedy show.

It was like a dream. At first April didn't want to believe it, but then again, she was talking to the air. Also if this was true, then it would explain the increase in mistrust around her. It's no wonder the few friends she had didn't even want to be near her: She'd gone insane.

"Did that all really happen?" April gasped, continuing to watch events unfold in the mirror.

"I'm afraid so. You were put under the Shadow Carnival's spell," Jane explained, feeling guilty about the situation. As the image faded from the mirror, April stared into her reflection, overcome by a mixture of feelings, guilt, disgust, and fear.

"Peggie and Zack need your help, April. They saved you. Without them you wouldn't be here right now," Jane said. April pondered her options.

"So this all happened because of that circus?" April stared at the empty space where Jane's voice was coming from.

Jane had become aggravated because the conversation was dragging. "Yes. Now will you help us?" April fell silent for a moment. She needed to absorb the absurdity of the situation.

"Just this once," she replied. Jane brightened up and eagerly held April's hand so that she could lead the way ... or rather to make sure she wouldn't run away.

"Thank you, just this once will do." Jane said gratefully. She pulled on April, giving her no choice but to follow behind.

The two of them rushed out of the bathroom, completely oblivious to Janette's presence. They made a sharp turn down the hall, rushing past the crowds of people approaching the sealed theater. April gripped her hand tightly around the handle and pulled with all her might.

Mimi was still singing from inside:

Don't you know I'm deeper than the ocean blue?

Say you love me! Hey, hey!

When April's fingers began to feel sore, she let go of the handle.

"How am I supposed to do this?" April asked, whining and shaking her hands as if that would make the pain go away.

"You're going to have to use your magic," Jane said.

April's jaw dropped, "Magic? You can't be serious?" With that Jane grabbed April's hand and her hand gripped the handle once again.

Jane explained. "It's the only way to open the door. It was sealed with magic. So now you have to unlock it with magic."

April still thought this was ludicrous. "I don't have any magic powers, and I can't do that." Her claim was another surprise to Jane.

"You can't do magic?"

"No, because I'm normal."

Was April lying? Was she in denial? Did she really not notice what she did in the bathroom? Is she ignorant of her abilities? Whatever the reason for this, Jane decided to instruct April on how to use her magic to open the door.

"Just picture the door opening. Picture it being light. Picture it opening without the slightest problem. Picture the door responding to that desire. Feel the door opening. Then open it," Jane said calmly.

April rolled her eyes. "I must be crazy." She imagined the door opening, just as Jane said. This time around she gave the door just a small nudge. Almost as if it had a change of heart, the door opened. The light from the outside poured into the theater. Someone from the audience noticed the light cast along the floor.

"The door's open," a voice cried, and he rushed out of his seat. Everyone followed suit, pushing each other out of the way as they all tried to rush down the stairs. April gasped and dove out of the way when she saw the crowds stampeding toward her. She swore that she could feel the ground shake as the crowd continued to flow out in a panic.

"What? Hey! Who scared my audience away?" Mimi demanded, stamping her foot and her face burning red.

"Zack, let's go," Peggie urged, getting up from her seat and bolting toward the door.

"Right, let's get her!" Zack cried. He rushed down the stairs toward Mimi.

Peggie screamed, "What? Zack, no! Let's just run away."

"As if I'll let you! Boys—get 'em!" Mimi ordered, and her two henchmen charged at them. Peggie screamed as she ran toward the door but got caught by the one of the bouncers.

"Come here! What Mimi wants ... Mimi gets," the first bouncer said. Peggie struggled as he dragged her by her arm.

"Let me go!" she cried. She placed her free hand on the man's back, spewing a thick mist from her hand. The first bouncer yelped as he shivered from his ice-covered back.

Mimi's jaw dropped at the sight of Peggie's magic. Just then the second bouncer fell down the stairs upon being struck by a bolt of lightning that illuminated the room. A clap of thunder followed.

"I'm going to unfreakify all of you," Zack said. His palms surged with building electricity. He aimed at the bouncer that was after Peggie.

"Peggie, move!" he warned a second before unleashing another bolt of electricity. Peggie dove behind a wall. Flashes of light and the blast of thunder filled the room.

To his surprise, Mimi shielded her loyal henchmen with her body. She blocked the bolt with her arms as if she had a shield. Sparks flew off of her when she took the hit, remaining unfazed by the attack.

Peggie and Zack were astounded by Mimi's immunity to the spell. It was lightning, after all. How could that not hurt?

"What are you guys doing? Just run!" April shouted from beyond the doorway.

The first bouncer finally recovered. This time he grabbed both of Peggie's arms and lifted her into the air. Peggie kicked her feet, anxiously trying to wriggle loose.

"April, help her!" Jane demanded.

"How?" April cried, on the verge of panic.

"Magic! You know how to do this," Jane reminded her. The first bouncer carried Peggie further into the theater.

April raised a fist to her face and stared at it intently. She was amazed to see it ignite but not burn. It felt more as if she were wearing a warm, toasty glove. April's eyes narrowed as she stared at the bouncer's back, painting a target in her mind.

She broke into a full sprint and pulled her arm back. As she closed in, she threw a punch into the man's back. A small explosion of flames and smoke shot from April's fist. The bouncer cried in pain from the rock-hard impact and searing flames. Peggie felt the flames brush by her when the bouncer dropped her. He fell onto his hands and knees, breathing heavily.

April ran to Peggie's side and helped her up as she yelled to Zack: "C'mon, let's go already!"

"She can't be that tough," Zack insisted and prepared another bolt of lightning.

Mimi tried to march up the stairs like a soldier, clenching her fists, with her eyes set on Zack. He backed away and released another bolt from his hands. Mimi blocked it with her arm. Sparks flew around her as if she were walking into a fire.

Zack lost his confidence when Mimi approached. Her pace quickened into a charge. She pulled her fist back, ready to swing, but Zack stopped his attack. He bolted further up the stairs, and Mimi swung her powerful fist, but it collided with a chair, causing the entire row to shift over. The chair at the other end flew into the wall and shattered into several pieces. Zack stared at the large dent in the wall with his mouth gaping.

Mimi screamed. "I've had enough of Dodie's meddling. You tell her that if she gets in my way again, I'll snap her in half. But not until after I rearrange your bones." She charged again.

Zack ran down an aisle in an attempt to go down the other side but was blocked the by the second bouncer, who was ready for him. Standing like a football player, he eagerly awaited Zack's arrival.

"Crap!" Zack cried as he stopped in his tracks.

"Good boy! Don't let him get away!" Mimi said, coming out of the aisle of chairs. With that April charged with another flaming fist and punched the second bouncer in the stomach.

As the bouncer keeled over, Peggie shouted to Zack, "This way!"

Zack made another trip through the aisle, and they all regrouped on Peggie's side. Mimi's face turned blood red when she reached for the nearest bolted chair and ripped it out of the floor.

"Come back here!" she screamed and chucked the chair across the theater.

They narrowly escaped the chair, which crashed into the wall. The three of them bolted out of the theater and ran down the hall through the crowds of people. Mimi burst through the other door and followed suit, pushing confused people out of the way.

Jane moved a trash can in Mimi's way and tripped her, falling flat on her face. The three dashed through the lobby and made their escape through the exits. Mimi got up and scanned the area for them. When she couldn't find them, she threw a tantrum.

"Stupid! Jealous! Wannabes!" she screamed, stamping her feet in fury while her loyal henchmen caught up to her.

CHAPTER 10

The Cost of Beauty

LATER THAT night Mimi was in a rundown apartment room. The wallpaper was coming off, and the lavender bricks showed through. Pots and pans were left out along the kitchen counter, the couch cushions were coming apart as if mauled by a dog, and the floor was bare cement.

Moaning emanated from behind the couch. It was Mimi on the floor, groaning and holding her stomach. "C'mon, Mimi. You can do this— ooh." She winced trying to slowly pull herself onto her knees. "Just a few more minutes ... then you can eat. It's only five more than yesterday's wait. Ah ... remember, we're not thin enough. That's why ... that's why no one wants to hear you sing." She muttered to herself as she glared at the energy bar in her hand. Her stomach caving in from anticipation of the chewy goodness of the morsel of food.

The ticking of the timer on the floor seemed to get longer and longer. What felt like ages passed as she held on to her noble determination to starve herself. Mimi glanced at the timer: Only a minute to go. "C'mon, almost there ... almost there ... almost ..." she muttered. She focused intently on slowly raising the bar to her mouth.

The timer flooded the room with the sound of beating bells. Mimi tore off the wrapper and wolfed the bar down, taking large bites and half chewing her food before swallowing it. She devoured the few bites in mere seconds, then sighed with relief, grabbed the timer, and rewound it as she clutched it in her hands.

This time she waited another five minutes. She placed the timer down on the ground before her and stared at it. She rocked back and forth as she waited, humming a string of incoherent tunes. She waited and she waited until finally the timer went off again.

This time Mimi got up and ran to the restroom. She flipped the light switch to the grime- and rust-covered bathroom. In one graceful motion, she flipped the lid to the toilet, assumed the position, and shoved her hand down her throat. With her extended finger in her warm, moist mouth, she jabbed her uvula. Her stomach convulsed, the stomach fluids traveled up her esophagus, and she regurgitated the foul yellow liquid into the bowl.

With broken chunks of what was her meal floating in the corn-colored water, Mimi flushed the toilet, banishing those evil calories to the far reaches of the sewer system. After that, Mimi washed and scrubbed her hands furiously in the sink, cleansing herself of the sin of food consumption. She took a deep breath and sighed with relief as she flipped her hair in front of the small mirror.

"See? You lost like ... a whole pound already." She smiled as she posed in celebration. However, when Mimi felt her thighs, this soon changed. She looked at her thighs and then back into the mirror as if to compare. Her face was consumed by doubt.

"Or maybe not." She gasped on her way to the toilet for an emergency second purge into the toilet.

After rewashing, Mimi reexamined herself, expecting to see instant results in weight loss. Unfortunately, she was disappointed because this is not how things work. She looked at her thighs and became stressed.

"Oh no, I'll have to eat only half a bar from now on. How could I be so stupid? It's no wonder they don't like me." She shed tears of shame. How dare she eat an entire energy bar? She should've known better, the fat pig.

Mimi walked back to the couch, sat in its flat cushions, and reflected on her heinous act.

She burst into tears. "I should've known; I'm an idiot. I should've known; eating all of it ... how? How could I go out there again?"

"Having trouble are we?" a familiar voice called from the kitchen. Mimi turned around to see Janette sitting on one of the bar stools.

Mimi's face lit up. "Janette! Why ... why are you here?"

"I wanted to see how you are doing. You know ... since you went solo." Janette was doing her best to hold back her resentment while joining Mimi on the couch.

"You know, this isn't really the home of a superstar, is it?" Janette said. The room lit up with the snap of her fingers.

Mimi looked around at the her dump of a home and hung her head, ashamed.

"No it isn't. I ... never knew ... it'd be so hard," Mimi replied, trying to hold back her tears. With that Janette removed a bag of fast food from her hat, took out a burger, and began to eat in front of her.

"Sounds like you've been through a lot. Do you want one?" Janette asked, offering the second burger.

Mimi eyed the burger for a moment, tempted to snatch it out of her hands. She politely rejected the food, but her stomach growled, furious at its denial of nutrition.

"Is it ... Do you have time to talk?" Mimi asked, looking at her with pleading eyes.

"Sure, tell me all about it," Janette said as a devious smile spread across her face.

Mimi went on about all that she had done recently. Janette kind of listened while continuing to eat in front of her.

"It's just not fair. What else can I do? I mean, I didn't look good enough before ... but now I'm pretty," Mimi said, catching Janette's attention.

"Before?"

"Yeah, before ... before we met," Mimi clarified and looking at Janette for a moment before returning her gaze to the floor.

"I still ... don't remember too much about that time, but I was ... I was always sad. I was fat. A lot of a people teased me for it. I even had this redhead oink at me." Mimi cried and paused to catch her breath, remembering girls making pig sounds whenever she walked by.

Janette glared hatefully at Mimi, thinking: So she's starting to remember now, is she? Leaving me wasn't enough for her. So now she has to do this to me?

"I tried out once," Mimi continued.

"For what?" Janette asked, dragged out of her own thoughts.

Mimi reluctantly continued. "For ... you know ... that show, *USA Idol*. They were here looking for people in this city. I ... wasn't good enough. They thought I was good, but ... it's stupid ... what chance did I have to eat at the same place they did? They were saying: 'The fat girl was good, but we can't sell her.'" As she repeated those words, they stung. She could hear the judge's voice so clearly.

Janette challenged her logic: "How did you know it was you they were talking about?"

Mimi sighed, "I was the only fat girl there. And I was never invited onto the show. Before that, whenever I came home, I'd sing every day. I'd sing to whatever tunes were on the radio. But not after that. It's been a while since I sang like that. Will ... will I ... will I ever be good enough?" Mimi wept, letting all the tears flow. A moment of silence passed.

"You know what? I'll help you," Janette said. She got off the couch.

Mimi looked up at her through her tears and hair. "You will?"

Janette's fiendish grin stretched across her face once more. She grabbed hold of Mimi's hand and held it reassuringly between her palms. "Sure, I'll help jumpstart your career. After all, I care about you, Mimi. I want to hear you sing."

Mimi's face immediately lit up at the words "I want to hear you." She stood up from the couch and hugged Janette tightly with renewed hope.

"I don't deserve someone like you," Mimi said gratefully.

"No. No you don't," Janette muttered as Mimi detached herself and wiped away the tears, smearing what was left of her makeup.

"So what are you going to do?" Mimi asked, her face brimming with excitement.

With that, Janette removed her hat and pulled out a small model of a stage. "First of all, you don't have a proper stage. Will this be to your liking?" Janette asked, egging her on as she held out the stage.

Mimi looked closely at the stage, as if examining the smallest grain of dust.

"No," she replied in disgust.

Janette was shocked. "What? Why? What's wrong with it?"

Mimi's jaw dropped, she couldn't believe that it wasn't obvious. "It's too small. How do you expect me to fit on there?" Mimi whined, stamping her foot.

Janette looked away, shaking her head as she muttered, "Perhaps I overdid it with you."

"What?"

"Nothing. I mean it's not big yet. Right now I'm asking if you like the *look* of it?" Janette saw the light bulb go off in Mimi's head.

"Yes I do. Now all I need is an audience," Mimi said. She placed her hands on her hips and posed as she envisioned her dream concert.

"The advertising shouldn't be hard. I'll set up flyers all over," Janette offered.

"No need," Mimi interrupted. "I'll take care of the audience. After all, they're going to adore me ... one way or another." A vial of her Burn serum appeared in her hand out of a puff of smoke.

Janette eyed the vial curiously. "What are you going to do with that?"

Mimi smirked. "Show the world just how brilliant I am." With that Mimi puckered her lips and smothered the glass with a big smooch, leaving red lipstick behind as if it were a stamp of approval.

The lipstick shimmered and vanished as the liquid turned into thick, dark purple sludge. With that Mimi walked over to the kitchen sink, removed the cork to the vial, and poured the sludge into the drain.

"Let's see them clean that." She smiled, tossed the vial aside, and nonchalantly made her way back to Janette.

"Done. Give it a few days to kick in and voilà! Instant fame!" Mimi gloated. Janette's interest was piqued by Mimi's concoction.

"Can't wait to see. Shall we?" Janette beckoned toward the door.

Mimi summoned her large sunglasses and placed them firmly on her face.

"Yes, let's," she replied, and the two of them marched out the door into the night. Mimi was humming a happy tune as she and Janette went off to scout for locations.

CHAPTER 11

The Beauty of Beauty

Z ACK WAS lying on his bed, reading a comic book, with a small bag of chips at his side. Clothes littered the floor in patches. Childhood action figures were lined up on the dresser. With only the lull of the ceiling fan's humming, Zack was drawn into one of his favorite comics.

While others would only read through the comic, Zack also paid close attention to the drawings. The boldness of the lines, the curves, the shapes, and the colors brought this fantasy world to life. Bringing life to his drawings was what Zack wanted most, so he studied the comic, hoping to learn some secret to the art of drawing.

As he got further into the story, he came across of a large drawing of the main character: muscular and gung ho man, the "ideal" image of how men "should be." The character never cried, and the character always wore a big cheesy smile as he fought the forces of evil. Zack couldn't help but feel a tad envious of the character's exaggerated physique, believing this is how men are expected to look.

Zack compared his arm to the character's and mumbled, "Guess I need to start working out. I'm not magically going to look good just sitting on my ass. Because I do, though, it might never happen."

When his cell phone beeped, he reached into his pocket, pulled out his phone, and swiped his finger across the screen to navigate to his messages. "Of course," he said, grumbling.

Zack tossed the phone to the side. It was opened up to the New Wayton's social media app. Several comments were posted on Zack's Web page and also several of his cartoon drawings. Some of them were of harmless anthropomorphic animals. The comments section of his Web page was littered with unwarranted anonymous insults. Most of them came from the day before when he had an argument with his harassers in the comments section. It was overflowing with responses that said things like: "How old are you again?" "How can you still be drawing this shit?" "Fur fag!" ... and a myriad of other insults directed at him.

He reached for a stack of paper, grabbed a pencil, and started to draw, starting with a torso, then vague limb shapes. He made a mistake with a crooked line, erased a little, and redrew it. He lost track of time trying to get the face of his made-up comic book hero right. He had to make several retries with the lines and curves, leaving eraser smudges all over the paper. They made it appear as if gray clouds or smoke was hovering around the character.

"Hey, Zack?" a young girl asked when she knocked on the door.

"What is it, Cassie?" Zack replied, not even bothering to get up and open the door. Cassie, a small, bright, green-eyed girl sporting a baseball cap, opened the door as she held some type of plush toy in her arms.

"Dad said he's bringing pizza home. What do you want on it?"

"Mushrooms and olives."

Cassie gagged. "Vegetables? You're gross!"

Zack didn't respond as he continued drawing. Cassie crinkled her nose and grunted at the lack of attention.

"So what are you drawing?"

"Justice Man," he replied with agitation.

"Oh, a superhero! Let me see! Let me see!" Cassie pleaded, looking over his shoulder. "Hrmm."

"What?"

Cassie looked at a wall covered in drawings featuring more cartoon characters, some of them anthropomorphic animals.

"I like those better."

"Of course you do," Zack said, grumbling. "You're a kid."

"What does that have to do with it?"

"Everything. You don't know what you're talking about because those pictures are bad."

Cassie couldn't understand this. "No they're not. I like them, I really do."

"Those are kid pictures. If I ever want be taken seriously as an artist, I have to make more grown-up things."

"But what's so grown-up about superheroes?"

"For starters, they ... uh ..." Zack trailed off since this was actually a good question.

Cassie tilted her head. "Yeah?"

"Cassie, just leave!"

She grunted and addressed her plush toy, a robot-like creature wearing a dark red police cap and a princely outfit: "Come on, Mr. Sentinel. Zack's being a jerk," she said and stormed out of the room.

He continued to draw, mumbling to himself. "This drawing is better ... it has to be," he said. He put down the pencil and returned to his comics.

"So what exactly are these artists doing to make them look so good? Do I just need to practice, or is there something I'm not getting?" He looked over the artwork again and pondered, as if there was some strange riddle hidden in it.

"Pizza's here!" Cassie chimed, appearing in the doorway for a brief second before scurrying toward the dining room. Zack set his things aside, got up from his bed, and stretched his back before going to meet everyone at the table.

As he came around the corner, his father, a thin, glasses-wearing man, was placing boxes of pizza on the brown wooden table. He opened the first box, revealing a fresh, hot, steaming pizza. Cassie grabbed the first slice and cut it into smaller bites with a plastic knife and fork.

Zack opened the second box, pulled off a slice, and stretched the melted web-like cheese, as if the pizza wanted to remain whole.

"How was work, Daddy?" Cassie asked in between bites. Mr. Styles grinned, showing his pearly white teeth.

"We're reworking the schedule for our shows today."

"Oh, does that mean you're getting a new one?" she asked excitedly.

"Yep. You will like this, Cassie. It's going to be about a witch who has gotten very popular lately," he replied happily after taking a bite of pizza.

"Oh! Oh! Is it a show about Candi?" she asked, getting pumped for the new show. Mr. Styles took a sip from his glass of water.

"It'll be on in a month. We'll be announcing it on TV tomorrow." He set the glass down with a smile.

Cassie gasped, "It is, isn't it?"

Zack asked, "Isn't Candi that picture book you still read?" wondering why she would still be reading such a book.

"Yeah, Candi is awesome. She's fun and kind, and she has this really cool cat that can turn into big cats. She helps the land of Sweet Tooth with the all the candy that she makes. Like this one time she used taffy to fix a bridge," Cassie explained enthusiastically.

"That's pretty cute," Zack agreed, intrigued.

"You mean cool. Everyone at my school likes Candi. She's the best."

Thinking about this brief description inspired some ideas in Zack for cartoon characters.

Mr. Styles took another bite and another sip of his drink and then another and another. The glass was emptied in a matter seconds.

"Wow, you were thirsty," Zack said with a smirk. Mr. Styles wiped the water off his mouth with his hand.

"I know, I've been like this all day. I keep drinking, but I never get enough," he said, aggravated with himself.

Cassie looked at her father closely. "Do you feel sick?"

"Maybe I am." He moaned while rubbing his forehead.

Zack finished his third slice of pizza, grabbed his glass, and made his way toward the fridge where he filled his glass with ice and water from the dispenser. The machine groaned as if these things were stolen from a bear. He pressed the glass to his mouth and let the ice-cold water pass his lips. He gulped it down, wiped his mouth, and placed his dishes in the dishwasher.

"Thanks for dinner, Dad." Zack said on his way to the living room sofa.

Cassie checked her pink cat-shaped watch.

"Hey, when does Mom come home?" she asked as if keeping track of her mother's curfew.

"Mimi closes tonight."

"Oh, okay. Wait … Who? That's not Mom's name."

"You're right, it isn't," he said, laughing. "Gosh, I'm out of it today. Think I'll sleep early tonight."

"I can't believe you got her name wrong," said Zack. "What would Mom think?"

"You'll know only if you tell her."

"I'll tell her," Cassie said.

Mr. Styles pointed at her like she was in trouble and with a smile said, "You're grounded."

"Shoot!"

Zack tuned in to the news on TV. A female reporter announced:

> Three months have passed, and the child of Mayor Dean Narrow is still missing. The mayor has raised the reward to twenty-five thousand dollars. Anyone with any information on the whereabouts of his daughter please call the number below.

"Not exactly the best time to be preoccupied with family matters," the male co-host chimed in, bringing to mind current issues. The female reporter continued:

> It really isn't. Citizens of New Wayton have been voicing their concerns over not just the increase in crime rate but also the sheer negligence the mayor has shown toward his duties lately. It has been noted that he has missed

the last three city budget meetings. A leak regarding the latest financial records shows the majority of the budget going to the police force, yet crime is as high as it has ever been.

The male co-host said:

According to anonymous sources, this is due to Dean Narrow's obsession with finding his missing daughter, with all resources going toward a case that has made no progress for months. They also report that investigations of several crimes unrelated to the mayor's missing daughter have been put on hold, dropped, or are making little progress because the mayor has assigned more resources to search for his daughter.

Zack began flipping channels. He thought that crime was probably on the rise because of the carnival, but no one would believe a circus would pull off all these kidnappings, let alone have magical powers. The audio from the TV was an unintelligible din as the channels changed.

"Oh, my show is going to come on soon. Channel 77, please," Cassie pleaded from the other side of the room. Zack punched in the number on the remote. The television switched to the station just in time for the "moral" of a children's story to be spelled out for the stupid.

"Remember, kids: Looks don't matter," the cartoon bunny said, staring out into the audience as the screen faded to black. A commercial immediately came on featuring Mimi.

"Looks *do* matter," she stated, smiling for the audience while holding a bottle of lotion in her hands.

"Oh, God, please don't jump out of the TV," Zack prayed, recalling Mimi's ridiculous antics. This time she was in a white dress, standing in front of a white backdrop to make a point. "Tired of being bland? Want to get people to notice you? Don't settle for the ordinary. Stand out!" she said, and with that line her outfit changed into a red dress. Some preschoolers must have been playing with glitter: The dress sparkled non-stop.

"Wow, she's pretty," Cassie thought out loud while Mimi did a few twirls and slow motion hair flips. A small window appeared in the corner of the screen, showing a close-up of a muscular male.

"Don't worry—we have men covered, too, with our top-of-the-line protein bars. So work out for that bod you've always wanted. Remember: It's all about looking good. The better you look, the better you are. All the more reason to get Burned," Mimi said with a cheesy smile. Cassie thought about this as she looked at her brother and then her Dad.

"How come you two don't look like that?" she asked.

What do you mean?" her father asked.

"Aren't all guys supposed to have muscles?" She though it was odd that her family didn't fit the commercial.

"Not everyone. In fact, not many people look like that," Mr. Styles explained.

Cassie frowned. "Yes they do. All the guys on TV do. And so do the guys who model underwear at the store."

"Well … that's different." He had little confidence she would understand how this works.

"Then why?"

"Cassie, not everyone has to look like that."

"So it doesn't matter how you look? Is the pretty lady lying?" she asked, confused.

"No, she isn't lying …" But Cassie interrupted him.

"So are *you* lying?"

"No, I'm not lying."

"I don't get it. How can looks matter and not matter at the same time?" Cassie cocked her head, trying to comprehend this conundrum.

"You'll understand when you're older." Mr. Styles had given up.

Cassie asserted her opinion as she lightly hammered her leg with her fist. "No, I won't because no one is explaining it right. I can't understand if you don't say it right."

Zack tried to intervene from the couch. "Cassie, leave Dad alone."

"No, no she's right. That was a terrible way to put it." Mr. Styles replied.

Cassie asked again: "So is the pretty lady right? Is looking good that important?"

"Cassie, it's good to look healthy. You see, it's normally healthy for men and women to exercise and not be too skinny or too fat. That's why people who look like that," he said, gesturing toward the TV, "look good to a lot of people."

This time Zack had a question. "Wait a sec. There's nothing wrong with being vain then?"

"Of course not. Not everyone is going to look the same. Some people just don't care about or choose not to look that way. Nothing wrong with it at all, especially if it encourages people to at least consider trying to be healthy, even if only for looks."

"I never thought about the healthy part until now," Zack admitted. The media and just about everyone normally says that looks don't matter, or that being vain makes you shallow.

Mr. Styles continued: "Men with muscles normally look good, and we have to exercise to look that way. Women exercise to help watch their weight. If anything, being at least a bit vain is a good thing, so long as someone doesn't go overboard with it."

Suddenly a commercial for *My Big Fat Life*, a reality TV show, began to play, showing a woman too obese to get out of bed.

"There, see what I mean?" Mr. Styles pointed to the screen and continued eating.

Zack examined himself, then recalled all the muscular superheroes and male models he'd seen.

Maybe I should start lifting weights, he thought to himself. He fantasized what it would be like to go up a few shirt sizes. Visualizing himself like that, he decided it would be a good look for him.

CHAPTER 12

A Free Sample

PEGGIE WAS on the living room sofa, browsing the Internet with her trusty laptop. The entire world was at her fingertips as she opened up window after window, occasionally watching videos that advertised fire extinguishers and chatting with friends in chat rooms using the famous language of the Internet consisting of initialisms like LOL.

The locks on the front door clicked loudly when the knob turned. Peggie's Mom came through the door carrying several bags of groceries. She had quite the talent: She had several plastic bags wrapped around individual fingers while her fist was clenched. Clearly this woman possessed an impressive amount of upper body strength for a dainty female.

"Mom, do you need help with those?" Peggie asked while her mother made her way to the table.

"Yes, it would be nice," Ms. Worth said, plopping the groceries onto the dining room table.

Peggie got up from her seat and rushed over to help sort the groceries and put them away. Bread went on the counter, milk in the fridge, and all things canned were placed in the pantry.

"There, if you're hungry, you can cook something," Ms. Worth said. She gathered up all the plastic bags and trashed them on her way to the bedroom.

"You have a date tonight?" Peggie asked, recalling that her mother doesn't work Sundays.

"Yes, I have to get ready," she yelled from the hall, rushing to pretty herself up. Moments later Peggie was back on the sofa when her mother eagerly came out of the hallway.

"Is this dress okay?" she asked nervously, looking at her with pleading eyes as she held up a slimming black gown with a low cut to advertise her breasts. Peggie was caught off guard by this question.

"Where are you guys going?" Peggie asked.

"To the movies—the one that wasn't attacked by hooligans."

"But ... do you really need to wear a dress for that? It's going to be dark inside the theater. Don't you think it's a bit excessive?" Peggie failed to comprehend her mother's thinking.

"I'm aware it's going to be dark, but other women will be there, so ... I have to do something to keep his attention."

Peggie looked off into space as if she expected to find a solution to her confusion. "That makes ... no sense."

"Fine, I'll try something more casual."

"You've been together for like two months. You don't need to make a first impression any more," Peggie pointed out. Her mother went into the bedroom and began shouting.

"That was Donnie. We broke up last week," Ms. Worth shouted from the bedroom.

Peggie was shocked. "What? You two got along fine. What happened?"

"He's a garbage man."

"So?"

"That would make me the garbage lady. I don't want to be garbage."

"Mom, you're being ridiculous."

"That's what he said ... and then he broke up with me."

"Mom, why do you keep doing this to yourself?"

Ms. Worth finally emerged from her room carrying what had to be half of her wardrobe. "Because I want the right guy," she said.

"But if one small thing is enough to ruin it for you, are you going to find him?"

"There's plenty of men. I just don't want to settle for something less."

"Mom—he had a job, and you liked him. Did the fact that he was a garbage man bother you that much?" Peggie was concerned about her mother's philosophy.

"Peggie, I want to marry someone who's respectable, like a doctor or a fire fighter. You'll understand this when you're older." Ms. Worth started holding up outfits to be evaluated. Peggie gave up on this argument and moved on to helping her mom pick out clothes.

"No. No. Maybe. No. It could work. No. No. They make clothes like that? No. That one! Try that one!" Peggie pointed to a white two-piece dress outfit with a buttoned-up long-sleeved coat and a long, slimming skirt.

"This one?" Ms. Worth wanted to know Peggie's reasoning for this choice.

"You want to stand out even in a theater, and it's more casual, but it still looks nice. So I think that one will work."

At that moment there was a knock at the door. Ms. Worth set aside her chosen outfit and went to answer the door.

She opened the door just a crack and asked who it was. In the short exchange of words, Peggie's mother received a bottle of lotion from the visitor, who left as quickly as she came.

"Who was that?" Peggie asked. Her mother eyed the cream-colored bottle with silver lettering.

"It was a girl handing out free samples." Ms. Worth replied and immediately headed toward the bathroom.

Peggie continued typing away on her laptop's keyboard while her mother was getting ready for her date. The computer made a bell-like noise, and another message popped up in her chat window. Peggie giggled as she read the message, but was startled seconds later.

"You guys are so fun to watch," a familiar voice said, giggling. Peggie yelped and accidentally dropped her computer on the floor. She looked around and saw a blurry silhouette sitting next to her.

"J-Jane? Don't do that!" she snapped, glaring at the ethereal entity.

"Sorry, I got bored." Jane said, laughing. Peggie retrieved her laptop and examined it closely.

"Peggie, is everything all right?" her mother called from the bathroom.

"Yeah, I'm fine. My computer scared me," she shouted back. She placed the laptop next to her.

"Jane—You can't be here when my Mom's around. What if she sees you?" she said, scolding her in a hushed tone.

"Don't worry, she can't see me. It's just that ... your powers are coming in, so you're starting to see me."

"Does that mean we'll be able to see what you really look like?" Peggie was anxious to see Jane's face.

"Eventually, yes, you will be able to see me. Especially if you're fighting the carnival, your powers will grow the more you use them." Jane herself was not excited.

Peggie hung her head low and sighed, "I ... still don't know if I should even be doing this."

"But you've done it so many times. That has to mean ..." Jane was attempting to persuade her.

"I didn't do it on purpose. They attacked me. I just wanted to get away. I never asked for any of this." Peggie's voice squeaked as she tried to keep her anger quiet.

"I ... I'm sorry. At the school, when April was freakified, I saw what you did. You tried to free the students, Peggie. That's why I want your help: You're able to do that kind of thing," Jane apologetically explained, looking away from Peggie.

"Can't you just find someone else? Like the police or something? I'm sure they'd do better than me. It's their job, you know." Peggie was hoping to weasel her way out of this crazy situation.

"I can't; I don't know who to trust. I can't hand out powers to just anyone who asks for them. Not everyone ... not everyone can be trusted with them. I'm still praying April doesn't go crazy with them." Peggie felt Jane's desperation, making it difficult to resist her pleas.

"Didn't you say that … we have magic? Shouldn't we be learning some spells? I don't know how you think we can do anything when we don't even know what we're doing," Peggie said.

"Well … I'm not exactly the teacher type, but I guess I could try to explain how to use different spells." Jane said.

"So why don't you?" Peggie asked, finding Jane's modest claim to be interesting.

"Most sorcerers rely heavily on their talents. Each sorcerer has a 'sorcery talent' which is a specific type of magic they are naturally gifted with using. In your case your talent is known as cryokinesis, which is ice magic, Zack's is elctrokinesis and April's would be pyrokinesis. Any magic you use involving ice will be much stronger compared to any ice spell they would try to use. If you want to defend yourself ice magic is the way to go. Sorcerers that acquire mastery over their talent always outdo someone who hasn't."

"So what you're saying—that I could use other spells, but they won't be as reliable?"

Jane shrugged. "Pretty much, but if you aren't going to help, then there's no point in teaching you. I wouldn't be that much help anyway. I'm only repeating what I know."

Peggie decided to switch topics. It had occurred to her that she'd never really got to talk with Jane.

"So … how long have you been dead?" Jane didn't think she'd ask this question.

Jane let out a meek laugh. "I've been dead for a really long time."

"So what have you been doing all that time?"

"Uh … I've kind of just been watching people, after seeing everything that's currently playing in theaters or plays. I've seen people be born, and I've also seen those same people die."

"Don't you have any other ghost friends?" Peggie asked, thinking there was some ghost community.

"You'd think I would, but I haven't seen a single other ghost."

"Really? I'd imagine there'd be tons."

"Maybe everyone in this city is just ready to move on."

"Then why are you still here?"

Jane took moment to think about what she would say. "The Shadow Carnival … they killed me. I just … I need something to be done about them."

Peggie was intrigued. "What do you mean? You've been around for a really long time, but the carnival …" She was interrupted by a high-pitched squeal coming from the bathroom, and she jumped from the couch.

"Mom! Are you okay?" Peggie rushed to the bathroom door but found it locked. She could barely hear the shower running over her mother's cries. Peggie violently shook the handle to no avail.

Jane stuck her head through the door and gasped. "Peggie get in here! You need to cool her off."

Peggie's heart skipped a beat, and her body tensed. *Is she on fire?* was the first thing she thought as Peggie backed away from the door. She raised her hands, and mist spewed from her palms as a CD-sized ball of ice formed in the air.

"Open, damn it!" she cried as she threw the ball at the door. With a loud crash, the door swung open, and pieces of ice and broken wood fell to the floor. Her Mom was sitting in the bathtub and crying, with the shower soaking her. Her arms and face were a dark red, her skin was cracked, and blood was beginning to show through her cracked skin.

"Mom!" Peggie screamed as she ran to her side. The redness was spreading across her arm as it steamed. The only thing Peggie could think to do was to douse her mother with her ice magic. Peggie threw her hands out, and a high-pressure, thick, white cloud enveloped her mother almost instantly.

Peggie felt the temperature in the air drop, and fortunately, her mother's screams began to subside, so Peggie eased up the blast. While the mist cleared, Ms. Worth breathed heavily. She was still red all over, with thin, clear bits of ice clinging to her skin and she was still in pain. Salty tears rolled down her face and burned as they seeped into the red wounds, mixing with the blood, and dripping onto the floor.

Peggie immediately whipped out her cell phone and frantically dialed for help, on the verge of tears herself.

"Hello, I need an ambulance please. My mom ... was burned. Her skin's all cracked and ..." Peggie began to sob as the assistant at the other end tried to calm her down and asked for their location.

Jane was horrified by the sight of Peggie's mother and looked around for the cause of the damage. She searched the counter and noticed the cream-colored bottle with silver lettering. The bottle explained what happened right there on the label: Burn.

Peggie continued to talk to the assistant, who told her help was on the way. Peggie was soon asked if there was a fire. "N-no," she replied, "there wasn't a fire o-o-or a-anything like that ... Chemical? I don't know, I just want someone to help her."

Upon hearing this, Jane got up next to Peggie, and in a hushed tone, she spoke into her free ear: "Peggie, it was Mimi. The Shadow Carnival did this."

CHAPTER 13

The Turning Point

THE NEXT day, Peggie texted Zack to meet with her and Jane during lunch at school. She wanted to talk about the Shadow Carnival, more specifically about how to stop them. As it turned out, Peggie's mother was not the only woman who suffered severe burns from beauty products. There was no doubt in Peggie's mind that this was the work of Mimi, but for Peggie that wasn't the worst bit of information.

Lunch had just begun, and Peggie had packed her own lunch for school. She didn't care about the strange and mocking looks she got from other students throughout the day. She didn't have the time to wait in those ridiculous lines when she had an important meeting.

Peggie marched through the halls and into the cafeteria, immediately sought out Zack, and joined him at the table by the missing persons board. Zack gave her a warm greeting but was alarmed by the cold and hateful look on her face.

"Whoa. Peggie, what's wrong?" Zack asked, completely surprised and almost afraid to find out what put such a timid girl in a foul mood. She opened up her lunch bag and slapped her meal down on the table in front of her.

She looked at him sternly. "Help me stop the carnival."

Zack's jaw dropped, "W-wow, okay. Yeah, of course I'll help. They're bad news to begin with, but why the change in attitude?" Peggie took a bite of her lunch and chewed, as if venting her fury on an innocent sandwich. Zack saw Jane's blurry silhouette float over to their table.

"Hi Jane, do you know what happened with Peggie?"

"Looks like I can't surprise you guys any more. As for Peggie, she has every reason to be angry."

Peggie sipped a swig of chocolate milk from a carton, took a deep breath, and explained. "I want the carnival gone ... forever. I want them gone because ... they hurt my Mom."

Zack's eyes widened. "They did what? How? What happened?"

Jane filled him in while Peggie continued to eat her sandwich. "Mimi's beauty products are some sort of acid. It burns the skin it touches really, really badly. Peggie's Mom will be in the hospital for a while."

Zack never would have guessed that Mimi was selling acid, let alone that any of this madness was really happening.

"It's no wonder you want to fight them now," he replied, understanding completely.

Peggie looked down at the sandwich before her. "It's not that I want to fight them. I just want them gone. Whether they move to a different city or get locked away, I don't care. I just want them gone, especially Janette."

"Why her?" He was puzzled as to why Mimi wasn't the target of her aggression.

Peggie looked straight into his eyes and said: "Because she did it. My Mom said 'a girl with a top hat' was promoting the product with free samples. She ... she came straight to my house. She wanted to hurt us. That's why I can't forgive her." Peggie shrieked and her muscles tensed up at the thought. Jane averted her eyes from Peggie, feeling guilty for getting her involved.

"Indeed. I have to say, I'm relieved to not be the only one who questions Janette's motives." A voice interrupted, causing the trio to immediately search for the uninvited guest.

A small girl with cotton candy pink hair stood before them, carrying a laptop at her side. Jane gasped. "Dodie!"

"Is she from the carnival, too?" Zack asked.

Dodie said: "You can all calm down. I'm not here to cause trouble. In fact ... I'm here to help."

Peggie glared at the girl, unwilling to take any chances. "Are you from the carnival?"

"As matter of fact, I am. I'm beginning to wonder why I even agreed to join. Anyhow, I didn't come to make small talk. You're upset with Mimi's Burn products, correct?" Dodie asked, skillfully redirecting the conversation.

"Yes." said Peggie.

Dodie opened up her laptop and drummed away at the keys. "Then it's best that I tell you she has done more than that. I suggest you all stop drinking tap water. It's been poisoned."

"Poisoned? But ... Mimi would never do that," Zack said. Dodie just smirked triumphantly.

"You just proved my point. You know Mimi is crazy, and she has sent several women to the hospital. Please explain why you should defend her?" Dodie asked, giving him a probing glare.

"She ... she's not that kind of person," Zack said, only to be chewed out by Peggie.

"Not that kind of person? She burned my Mom! We just talked about this. What are you saying?"

Zack stared at her, feeling the guilt eating at him from inside. "I ... I don't know. I don't know what I'm talking about."

Dodie smirked and took a seat at the table. "Exactly, because you're being poisoned. It seems Mimi's serum for men has brainwashing elements. Oddly enough, some trace amounts of steroids have been detected as well."

"S-steroids! She's brainwashing people with steroids?" Peggie asked, as this was among the most ridiculous things she'd ever heard.

"Actually, she's brainwashing only men," Dodie clarified. "After continuous exposure, they will experience a trivial amount of muscle growth as well as an increase in affection toward Mimi. The poison seems to be an alteration to her products directed toward males. As it turns out, she just began advertising her concert on TV. My guess is she's doing all of this just to get a crowd. For the female side of things, my assumption is it's some half-baked reason for revenge. Or perhaps she is trying to rid herself of female competitors."

"Where is the concert?" Peggie asked. She felt the atmosphere becoming heavy.

Dodie drummed away at her keyboard some more. "She'll be at the Wayton football stadium, off of Fire and Grudge Road. She'll be there Friday night, so until then I suggest you have your friend stock up on bottled water."

Zack eyed Dodie with suspicion. "Why tell us this? Aren't you from the carnival as well?"

Dodie scoffed at this question, "That doesn't mean we have a 'relationship.' I'm busy working on purifying the city's water supply. That's why I'm requesting that you stop her. I have every reason to believe that Mimi may intend to go global with her plan. She would become a de facto dictator. Having about half of the human population under control is a large amount of power to wield. Also, if one gender becomes completely enthralled by her, it means no more humans ... *ever*. In addition, Mimi would either just poison the water again or do something even more absurd to retaliate."

Zack scratched his head, "Wow ... you really thought this out didn't you?"

Dodie straightened her back to make herself taller as she replied. "Of course. Who do you think is the one in charge of all the business arrangements?"

Peggie smiled. "Thank you, Dodie. You don't know how much this means to me."

Peggie began to believe that Dodie must be different. She seemed reasonable, right? Perhaps they could trust her. Just maybe she'd help them run the Shadow Carnival out of town.

But Dodie stabbed Peggie with a cold and resentful glare. "Please, I'm doing this for the sake of sensibility, though I'm glad to hear that you're grateful. I don't get enough recognition. Though I suppose it's only natural for … children to admire those more capable than them."

Peggie's mouth dropped. "Did you just … insult me?"

"Glad to see you didn't inherit your intelligence from your mother," said Dodie. "Honestly, taking things from people you don't know? That level of naiveté should be illegal." She closed her laptop and got up from her seat.

Zack was infuriated as he got up from his seat. "You can't talk to her like that!"

Dodie brushed her hair out of her face. "First Amendment. Glad the education system is broken as always. Anyway, I need to put on the final touches to the antidote. While I do that, you all better prepare to confront Mimi. She may be an incompetent airhead, but she is still dangerous, so with that I wish you luck."

Having given them her advice, Dodie left the group. She disappeared into the crowd with her chest out as if to look bigger. Despite her being a pink-haired child, it seemed as if people were too caught up in their conversations to even acknowledge her presence.

Peggie couldn't believe who she just met. "Wh-what was that about?"

"That was Dodie," Jane warned. "She's another one of the head carnies who run the carnival. She's smart and seems sensible, but as you can tell, she's just arrogant and rude. No matter what she says, she's crazy just like the rest of them." Jane scanned the crowd to make absolutely certain Dodie had indeed left.

"So now what?" Zack asked with a sigh. "Do we get April's help, too?"

Peggie brightened up because she liked the sound of that idea. "Yes, three people is better than two, right? Mimi's like, super strong isn't she? We're going to need all the help we can get, if we're going face her."

While the three of them were agreeing to try to get April's help, April was looking for a place to eat her lunch. She walked down the aisles carrying a tray of the blandest pizza on the planet until she spotted a table that still had some room left for her.

She squeezed her way onto the bench and put her tray down. Just as she was about to begin eating, she recognized some of the students at the table. They were all staring at her, some with fear, others with resentment. April felt like she was chained down by an unexplainable weight. Some students got up and moved to a different table. Who could blame them? They thought of her as some lunatic that needed to be arrested. If the evidence hadn't disappeared, she would have been behind bars.

"They don't matter," April mumbled to herself and took a bite of the cardboard pizza. What the heck is the Shadow Carnival? If it wasn't for them, I wouldn't be in this mess. It wasn't my fault I went crazy. Why am I taking the blame? she wondered while swigging strawberry-flavored milk. "I just want to forget about this. It's not like I could actually do something about it anyway," she muttered under her breath, recalling the incident at the movie theater.

"April, there you are," Jane said cheerfully and planted herself next to the vexed girl. April noticed a faint blur sitting next to her, talking to her.

"Not you again," she grumbled. April crossed her arms and looked in the other direction, attempting to ignore her. To her dismay, Peggie and Zack also joined her at the table.

April rolled her eyes. "What do you guys want?"

Peggie began to feel anxious. "Well ... we want ... we want you."

"C'mon, Pegs, what happened to that fire a moment ago?" Zack asked, agitated by her sudden reversal.

"I'm trying," Peggie snapped, glaring at him with a hateful gaze.

With this, April's loose mouth stepped in. "Wow, even the princess has had enough of you. That's saying something."

Zack growled. "Do we really need her help?"

"You're asking me to help you again? I already helped you. Get someone else to do it!" Since April was still looking the other way, Jane moved into her sight.

"Look, April. Don't you hate the carnival too?" Jane asked, egging her on.

April grunted, then looked the other way, determined to ignore her. "Of course I do! That doesn't mean I want to get them back," she replied, grunting with agitation when Jane moved in front of her again.

"At least help us get rid of Mimi, April," Peggie pleaded.

April gave Peggie a cold look, "You mean that bimbo? Why? I never pegged you as the type to go after someone. There's no way you mean it anyway."

"Yes I do," Peggie snapped, raising her voice.

"No you don't," April insisted.

Peggie had enough of arguing with her. So with one sentence she was able to get April's attention: "*She hurt my Mom!*" April fell silent. She never would have guessed that something like that would actually happen.

"D-did she really?" April asked softly, guilt beginning to sink in.

Peggie tried to calm herself. "Yes, she has very bad burns. She'll need skin grafts for her face and arms. She was in so much pain. Her skin is cracked, and she said it hurts to move. I can't let them get away with it. Not this, not what they did to Mom."

April looked into Peggie's eyes and saw how serious she was, "Your Mom sounds ... important to you. Isn't she?"

Peggie nodded and her eyes glistened. "Isn't everyone's Mom?"

April's heart tore at the sound of that question. "I don't know. My foster parents are divorced" she replied.

Zack's eyes widened, "Did you say 'foster parents?'"

"Yes, I did—I'm adopted. Whoop-de-do! Gonna make fun of me now? Go ahead, I stopped caring," April said with a scowl.

"N-no, I just didn't think you were adopted is all," Zack said, desperately trying not to sound like a jerk.

"April, your stepdad's in danger, too," Jane said, thinking this would get her attention.

April's expression changed. "What do you mean, he's in danger?" she asked, finally interested. The three of them quickly filled April in on what Dodie told them.

April's eyes widened as it dawned on her. "He did say something about a 'Mimi' this morning. You don't think he's brainwashed, do you?" This was the first time anyone saw April actually get worried about something. She expected them to say it was only a joke, but they only nodded and reaffirmed her fear.

"It might not take full effect in everyone at once, but it will eventually," Jane explained.

April thought about this. "Things are already kind of shitty at home. The last thing I need is him leaving me to rot for some crazy bimbo."

After thinking long and hard, April finally replied, "Okay. I get it. I'll help you."

"Really?" Jane chirped excitedly.

"There's not much to my life; the last thing I need is to be taken care of by a brainwashed Mimi fan," she said. A bell went off over the intercom.

"Wow, lunch is over already?" Zack noted, amazed by how much time has passed.

April groaned. "Now I'm gonna go hungry. This is what I get for helping you? Thanks a lot!"

Peggie looked away. "Sorry about that."

The students got up from their seats and formed one large mass of bodies. They flooded the halls as if a dam had burst. Peggie and her friends agreed on a time and date to meet again before heading off to class.

As the day continued, classes seemed easy compared to what was to come. They had to be ready. They had to be prepared. This was the only thing they were concerned about. But the question was how.

CHAPTER 14

Melodrama

A FEW DAYS later, Peggie and her friends were sitting at a table, eating burgers from the fast food restaurant that was integrated into J-Mart, the supermarket. People constantly came in and out of the doors nearby. It was like as having a picnic next to a stream. It was much quieter than the school cafeteria in spite of the sea of people invading the store. Everyone living enjoyed the juicy burgers.

"You guys ready to find some clothes?" Jane asked after sitting quietly for several minutes. Peggie felt guilty about eating in front of her. "You know you could eat something, too, if you want."

Jane chuckled. "I would, but all that food would go right through me."

"How could you forget about that?" April asked cynically.

"I was just trying to be nice," Peggie said.

"Now that we're done, exactly what kind of clothes are we looking for?" Zack asked.

Jane said, "It has to be something you can fight in. It'd be no good for me to enchant them if clothing gets in the way."

April raised an eyebrow at their ethereal friend. "So you can really make armor out of ordinary clothes?"

Jane nodded. "Yes, I did it several times when I was alive. It's easy when you know what you're doing. Trust me, you're going to need it. I'll be sure to put in a last defense spell."

"A what?" Peggie asked uneasily.

"If the clothes rip or break in any way, you need to call it quits and run. The armor will only prevent *one* lethal attack."

The three of them left the food court and followed the ghost to the maze of shops and looked around, trying to find reasonable clothes.

"Something that'll be good to fight in. Hmm. Maybe ... some shorts?" Peggie suggested. She had come across a shelf with several colors of shorts.

"As long as we don't look stupid, I'm fine with it," April said with her arms crossed.

"You might not get to choose," Zack pointed out. He rummaged through shirts hanging off the many racks.

Jane zoomed around in the air, scanning the area for good pieces of clothing. "Ooh!" she cried as she made her way to a rack full of jackets. She grabbed what appeared to be a jean material vest and waved it around. "I think this could work out great with those shorts."

Peggie took notice and brightened when she saw the vest. "Oh, that would look nice."

"Find any gloves?" April asked, intrigued now that the girls had gone into wardrobe mode.

"Jane, you're a ghost. Stop levitating things in public," Zack shouted back at her when he caught her holding clothes.

"Oops, I forgot," Jane said and dropped all of the clothes onto the floor just as a group of customers passed by the aisle.

Zack pulled a wifebeater tank top off a nearby stand. "What about this?"

April took one look and rolled her eyes. "Please, you got nothing to show off. It'll just look stupid on you."

"Gee, thanks," he said and grumbled while continuing to look around in the men's section.

"Don't be too hard on him, April," Jane said, chuckling.

April began her search through a pile of accessories. "He'll get over it. He's a boy; he can take it."

Zack looked over at the pictures of the muscular male models advertising shirts and underwear and couldn't help but feel inadequate.

Peggie saw the look on his face. "Are you feeling okay?" she asked.

"Yeah, I'm fine," he replied with bitterness and put the shirt back.

Jane was feeling guilty. "Zack, we didn't mean to make fun of you."

"No it's not that; I'm fine," he insisted and went further into the men's section.

Peggie said to April, "Maybe we should apologize?"

"For what? It's not my fault he gets upset about it." April sneered as she walked off by herself.

"Why do you have to be like that?" Peggie shouted after her, only to be ignored when April disappeared into another aisle.

"If this is how it's going to be, I don't know how we're supposed to stop the carnival," Peggie said. She looked back and forth between the paths her friends took.

Jane came to her side, and with a comforting voice she said, "It'll work out. You guys are all new at this is all."

"I hope so. Mimi is supposed to be super tough right? We'll need every bit of help we can get," Peggie was depressed at the thought of what would happen if Mimi was left alone.

Jane glanced over to where April disappeared and asked, "Do you have any clues why she's so sour?"

"No. Ever since I first spoke to her, she's been really mean."

"What did you say?"

"I think I asked her if she had a spare pencil. The lead was broken in mine, so I just wanted to borrow one."

"And?"

"She said no and just called me a princess. Then Zack got on her for being rude, and the two have been at it ever since."

Jane giggled at the thought. "Maybe they'll fall in love like in the movies."

Peggie looked baffled. "Are you serious?"

"No, but wouldn't it be fun if they did?"

"You're very ... strange for a ghost."

"Haunting houses is fun for only so long."

With that, Peggie's cell phone began ringing. She grabbed it and answered it.

"Mom? How are you doing?" Peggie asked urgently. Jane remained silent, trying to listen in on the call.

"Really? ... That's good ... Yeah, I hope to see you home soon ... Yeah, I'm doing okay," she said, bombarded by her mother's questions. She ended the phone call. "All right, I love you too. Bye."

"How's your Mom doing?"

Peggie smiled. "She's doing much better now. She says she might be able to come home in less than a week."

"Good to hear. Let's go catch up with the others. I bet they've got the clothes picked out by now," Jane flew further into the clothes department and Peggie scrambled after her.

But when they left, Mimi began walking through the aisles, carrying large bags filled with accessories and clothes and wearing a slimming black dress and her signature sunglasses.

As Mimi walked down the aisle, several passing males took notice. "Mimi? Is that really her?" "Love of my life, I've found you at last," some said. Mimi flipped her hair as she passed the gawking bystanders. She made her way toward the nearby makeup section. Some of the braver men followed her. No doubt this odd entourage raised many women's eyebrows, which made Mimi smile.

"Mimi! Is there anything I can get you? W-water? Something to eat?" one of the smaller lads said. As if by impulse, Mimi shoved a few of her bags onto him, which he gladly accepted. He turned around and smirked at the other guys, who glared at him furiously.

Another male, who happened to be an employee, approached Mimi the moment he saw her. "Are you looking for something in particular, Mimi? I can give you a discount—half off. Just say what it is, and I'll get it for you," he said.

Mimi played along with an obviously fake giggle. A nearby female customer was enraged by the sound of this. "Excuse me. Why is she getting a discount?" she bellowed in the employee's face.

The employee responded with a dumbstruck expression. "You know what? You're right. Mimi, you can take whatever you want. It's free!"

Mimi chuckled, "In that case ... everything! I want every last bottle of makeup you have. Make sure you check in back, too. No holding out on me, now!" She winked flirtatiously at the employee, and he sped off with a bright red face of delight.

"Are you serious?" the customer screeched. Mimi lowered her sunglasses and looked down on her.

"Of course I am. I have a show to put on. Unlike you, I have to look my best," Mimi said to the woman's face and gloating. The woman turned red with anger and wagged her finger in Mimi's face.

"Now you listen here, you skank!" the customer shrieked. As if that was the magic word, Mimi's fans grabbed hold of the woman, who let out a startled yelp.

"You can't talk to her like that," the man said, growling.

She struggled to get her tightly squeezed arm free from the man's massive hand. His grip felt as if she were tied to a truck. "Let go of me! That hurts."

"Then you better apologize to her," the man threatened. The woman exchanged glances with Mimi, who gave her an expectant look, as if she were downright better and always would be.

"I will do no such thing," the woman said, growling.

The man said to Mimi, "What do you want me to do with her?"

Mimi put a finger on her lip to think about it. "Find the biggest freezer here and lock her in it. Maybe it'll cool her down."

"Wow, you're so thoughtful," the bag-carrying worshiper said as the woman was carried away kicking and screaming.

Soon Mimi and her entourage were scooping makeup into bags that went in shopping carts. Several employees came with more shopping carts filled with makeup. Once the store was stripped of its beauty products and Mimi's Burn was put in its place, she headed for the exit with her chest out, waving to all of her fans that noticed her.

To the onlookers who gawked in amazement, this was the most absurd event ever seen in a store. Mimi flaunted her looks as she passed by all the women and walked through the automated doors. With just a simple hello, the male greeter let her and what had to be seven tons of makeup out the door. The air immediately filled with sirens when the scanners detected "stolen" goods. Back at the clothing center, this alarmed Peggie and her friends.

"What the heck is going on?" Zack thought out loud, about to pay for his bag full of clothes.

"I'll go look," Jane enthusiastically volunteered, being the most curious of them.

Peggie exchanged nervous glances with April and Zack, who continued to pay like good, law-abiding citizens. The cashier hurriedly gave them their receipts, but the alarms put her on edge.

With their newly acquired battle attire in hand, they headed toward the exits, giving Jane a chance to come back and find them.

Momentarily, the flying blur of a ghost returned to their side and reported: "You guys aren't going to believe this."

"Try me," April retorted. They listened intently as the alarms continued to blare.

"Mimi just came in and *stole* all of the makeup. She even took some people with her," Jane reported, feeling antsy as if they should do something about it.

"This is our chance. Let's get her," Zack suggested.

Peggie objected. "Wait! We still haven't enchanted our clothes."

"We won't have to if we get her now," April said. She and Zack dashed madly toward the checkout center, dropping their bags of clothes.

"Wait!" Peggie shouted after them as the two of them vanished behind a rack of clothes. Peggie picked the bags off the floor, straining her puny arms to carry all of their clothes.

The alarms turned off while Peggie walked to checkout. She passed the line of cashiers and met her friends by the automated doors. They had sheepish looks and were hanging their heads.

"Was she already gone?" Peggie asked.

"Yeah," Zack said, sighing with disappointment.

"You guys remember why we're making armor in the first place right?" Peggie asked.

April groaned. "I get it. It was stupid," she said. "Now can we get this part over wi- ... shit!" She began to hold her arm as a familiar sensation rose within her. She made a mad dash to the restroom leaving everyone else baffled by this sudden behavior.

"April? Where are you going?" Zack called after her, stunned as they all were by her sudden departure. When she got to the bathroom door, she stumbled and fell to her knees with a yelp. This immediately set off alarm bells for her friends.

"April," Peggie said, gasping. They all sprinted toward their sickly companion. April heard them calling and knew they were coming for her, but she couldn't let that happen.

With all her strength, April pulled herself up and went into the bathroom where she hugged the cold wall with her body. The muscles in her arms and legs twitched violently. April reached the sink and hoped to make it to the stall, but when her other leg gave way, the rest of her body began to twitch uncontrollably.

April fell to the floor with a thud, where she clenched her teeth in anger. Of all the times to have another seizure, it had to be one where her secret could get exposed.

Her three companions made it to the restroom entrance. Jane stopped Zack from entering as if it were a VIPs only party and followed Peggie inside.

"April, what's wrong?" Peggie yelped.

"Peggie you take care of her, Zack, and I will get an ambulance," Jane said, but when she tried to exit the restroom, she was stopped by April's plea.

"N-no! D-don't!" April growled as she attempted to get up.

Peggie knelt by April's side and frantically asked, "Is there anything I can do?"

"I'll get the ambulance," Jane re-announced and once again attempted to leave.

"No! They can ... they can't do anything," April hollered as the twitching began to subside.

"Why not?" Jane demanded to know, hurt by April's rejection of her help.

"Just … just give me a minute. It's going away." April panted. Her heart was still pounding from the attack.

"Are we getting an ambulance or not?" Zack's voice echoed from the entrance.

April sighed in aggravation. "You call them, and I kick your ass!"

"April … you're going to be okay, right?" Peggie asked, fearing that April had caught some deadly disease.

"Yes, I'm fine," April retorted, feeling vexed as she stood up, crossed her arms, and turned her back to them.

"April, what *was* that? What happened to you just now?" Jane asked, floating into April's view. April averted her gaze as she turned away from her, but Jane just kept moving to wherever she was facing.

April huffed. "Fine—I have epilepsy. You happy now?" Peggie and Jane exchanged glances.

"So you can't look at lights?" Peggie asked. She didn't understand much about the illness.

"No, that's not it. I … I get random seizures. Every once in a while my body freaks out for no reason. I know when I'm getting one because for me it starts as a small twitch. So I run to the closest place where no one can see."

"Isn't that dangerous though? What if you get a really bad one?" Peggie asked.

"If I ever get a really bad one, then that's it," April replied coldly.

"April … shouldn't you go see a doctor? They can help, can't they? They can make you better, right?" Jane urged, wishing for April to avoid a "bad seizure." Annoyed, April glared at Jane.

"Are you even listening? I told you they *can't*. It's genetic, so they can't just fix me. I was made broken. Okay?" April said. The two girls fell silent.

Zack, tired of waiting, entered the women's restroom.

"At the theater, did you leave because you were having an attack?" Zack asked because the possibility dawned on him.

Peggie gasped. "Zack, you can't be in here."

"Then let's go somewhere else," he said, annoyed by the girls' order of priorities.

"I second that. Maybe if we can find a good place to sit, April will feel better," Jane said optimistically. On that notion all four of them returned to the food court where they sat at the green table of the Tram Way burger shop. April was feeling stressed while all three of her teammates watched her closely as if they expected her to explode at any moment.

"You sure you're okay?" Zack asked, wanting to be sure.

April sighed in aggravation. "Yes, for the billionth time, yes. It's not like it happens every five minutes."

"Then how often does it?" Jane asked, taking this as good news.

"It's not as bad as it used to be. I get seizures around once a month or every other month. It's not like I could just write it on a calendar. The only warning I get is when I feel ... scared."

"Whenever you get scared it happens?" Jane asked for confirmation.

April rolled her eyes as if she had explained this many times before. "No, I get scared because it's going to happen. My chest gets tight and my heart starts to race. I feel like there's someone standing behind me, trying to choke me or holding a knife to my back. No one is actually there, of course, but ... I get the feeling that something bad is going to happen minutes or seconds before the seizure."

Peggie imagined herself in that situation, and the thought made her stomach turn. "That's awful. Do all the warnings come so late?"

April nodded. "I'm told other people receive better warnings than I do. Supposedly they are warned like a week in advance, so they can prepare for it. I always have to guess. I always have to figure out where the nearest bathroom is or someplace I can just get away from everyone."

"You mean so you can hide it, right?" Zack said.

April huffed. "It's not like having seizures is something to be proud of. Not that you would understand. You didn't have everyone call you a spaz or keep you from playing with them because they didn't want you spazzing out in the middle of kickball or some stupid shit."

Zack remained silent and felt guilty for bringing it up.

"So will it go away one day? You said it's getting better, right?" Peggie asked, picking up on this key fact.

April nodded. "That's what I was told. The doctors said that it's better to have epilepsy as a kid because you'll grow out of it. I'm not sure I believe them though."

"Don't talk like that. You just have to wait till you're older and it'll be gone," Jane asserted optimistically.

April huffed. "But I'm older now than I was then and it's still not gone. How much longer do I have to wait?"

Attempting to comfort her, Zack pointed out: "You're not an adult yet. We all still have some growing to do."

"Then there's no need to worry, then." Peggie was relieved to know the condition was temporary.

April rested her head on her hand. "That's not good enough." She grabbed her bag of clothes and got up from her seat. "Anyhow, I guess I'll go return my clothes."

"Wait a sec—what do you mean?" Zack asked.

April rolled her eyes, "I'm not stupid. Were you all were thinking that the sick girl shouldn't fight?"

"That's kind of a good point actually," said Peggie.

"See? Why did I even bother?" April said and headed toward the help center.

"That wasn't what we were thinking, though," Peggie argued.

"Doesn't matter," April replied.

Jane flew toward April and blocked her way. "We don't want you to go."

April sized up the blurry cloud from top to toe. "You know I could just walk through you, right?"

Jane was hesitant to argue with this. "Uh … but I still don't want you to go."

"Whatever." April scoffed only to have Peggie hold her hand to anchor her.

"April, please don't. I don't want you to leave either," Peggie pleaded.

"Yeah, your condition isn't enough of a reason for you to leave. It doesn't sound that bad," Zack said in agreement with the others.

April was astounded. "Wh-why would you want an epileptic girl to stay?"

Peggie looked away sheepishly. "Well … even though we did it to prepare for the carnival, I had fun hanging out with you today. I was hoping we could hang out again, you know ... for fun when we aren't doing carnival stuff." This left April with her mouth hanging open.

Zack threw in his two cents. "You know, April, you can go if you really want to, but I don't mind if you stay. I don't have anything against your epilepsy. We just wanted to make sure you are okay. Now—if it happens again—we know what to do next time."

"What if I get a seizure during a fight?" April asked with irritation.

Peggie replied: "You get warnings, don't you? Just let us know if you feel it coming on."

"Yeah, we can even have a code for it when it happens," Zack suggested. "You can yell something like 'pineapple'. That way any freaks within earshot won't know what you're talking about. We'll try to give you time to deal with it then."

Jane pitched in with her own optimism. "I can help too. I could find you a spot to rest, and when you're feeling better, you can help out again."

April looked away, trying to comprehend the situation. "I ... What is wrong with you people?" she finally blurted out.

Zack felt a bit offended. "What do you mean by that?"

"People ... People don't ... they ... ugh! This is dumb. What you're saying doesn't make sense." April exclaimed, becoming vexed.

"What's so dumb about saying that we want to help you out?" Zack asked, raising his voice.

"Because usually no one does," April said. "People don't help with *anything!*"

"I ... I'm sorry, I didn't mean to upset you," Peggie said apologetically in an attempt to diffuse the situation.

April fell silent for a moment. "No, sorry, you didn't upset me. I'm just confused. So can I just go home for the day? I'm tired, and people are staring."

Peggie saw that other hungry customers were looking in their direction. "Oh, uh, okay. Yeah we should definitely go home."

With that, April took the lead and began to guide the group toward the nearest exit, with Zack, Peggie, and Jane trailing behind.

"What the heck was that about?" Zack asked in a hushed voice.

"I honestly have no idea," Peggie replied.

Jane joined the conversation. "Do you think she just gets moody after one of her episodes?"

"Maybe," Peggie said and thought about it a moment. "Or it could be something else. Let's not talk about it anymore, though. That stuff is kind of personal to her, and I want to respect that."

With that they dropped the conversation. Even though April's emotional outburst was worrisome, they felt a bit closer to their former pain-in-the-side companion. A more important topic to think about was how exactly would they would deal with April if she had a seizure during a fight. After all, she might have only a few seconds warning before a seizure. The answer would elude them for the remainder of their trip home, where they would wait for their inevitable conflict with Mimi. Their hopes for survival in a fight with Mimi were up to Jane and her limited abilities to enhance their garments.

CHAPTER 15

Dress Rehearsal

TIME HAD passed, and it was the day of Mimi's concert. Many people had made plans for this day while they were succumbing to the effects of Burn. Mimi's concert was the topic of most conversations April had heard throughout the week.

April entered through a set of double glass doors that were decorated with posters of common house pet animals. People were sitting in chairs along the walls of the lobby. Some of them brought big dogs on leashes. Others brought smaller animals in portable cages. The lobby was filled with plenty of noise. The sound of cats constantly meowing with fear filled the air.

"Oh good, April, can you go in back and refill the food bowls, please?" the lady clerk asked, pointing to the back room.

"Yes I will," April replied with annoyance. She hauled the large bag over to the door and stood there at the door with her hands full.

"Uh … Are you going to get the door for me?" April asked.

"Hmm? Oh no, I can't … busy," the clerk replied as she continued flipping through a magazine.

"Oh for Pete's sake," she muttered, finding a spot to put down the bag. She started negotiating the complicated process of getting through the door. First she opened the heavy door, which took both of her arms to pull, then pinned it against the wall with her back, leaned over, and dragged the bag across the floor. While she did this, people just watched. They found it amusing.

Once the bag was in the doorway, April went through and closed the door to push the bag the rest of the way.

"Thanks for nothing!" she shouted, knowing she couldn't be heard through the door.

Inside was a hallway of dog pens. All were empty as if April had arrived just after a prison break. She traveled down the hallway, lugging around a large sack of dog food. She set the bag down along the wall and tore it open then went around and gathered up all of the food bowls to fill them up.

"Finally," she said with a relieved sigh. A door down the hall opened up and an African American man in a doctor's coat was standing in the doorway. The name Sean Day was written on the name tag clipped onto his coat.

"Oh April, can you help for a second?" he asked.

"Why? What do you need?" she replied with little energy.

"I just need you to help me medicate the cats," he answered.

"Don't you already have someone helping you?" April asked as she approached.

"I did, but she's pregnant and currently puking her guts out," he answered sheepishly.

"Of course. People actually doing their job? Just what was I thinking," she said sarcastically.

"Oh come on; it's a slow day. No need to get harsh," he replied while ushering her into the room filled with cat cages.

"Slow? When was the last time you've seen the lobby?"

"This morning, why?"

April paused for a moment. "You know there's like twenty people in there, right?"

Mr. Day opened one of the cages and took out a hairy white cat that was very frightened as it tried to escape. April grabbed the cat and pinned it down on the table as it continued crying.

"Ms. Hawford will take care of them." He blew off the observation.

"Uh, no. No she won't. She wouldn't even help me with the door."

"She probably had her hands full," he said. He got out a sterile needle for a syringe.

"I had my hands full. Stop it, cat! She was screwing around with a magazine."

"I'm sure it wasn't a magazine." He blew her off again as he prepared the syringe and got disinfectant ready. April growled in frustration.

"April, getting along with people is something that you're going to have to learn. I don't know why you always have to make an issue out of things, but it's something you're going to have to learn for when you're older," he said, lecturing April while he disinfected the area of injection.

"No, that's stupid. If I don't like someone there's a reason for it," April snapped.

"So you have a reason for hating everyone at school? Everyone?"

"I don't hate everyone, just … most people," April replied hesitantly. Mr. Day rolled his eyes.

"Seriously though, you need new employees, ones that will actually do their jobs," she insisted, hoping this time her point might sink in.

"Or maybe you just need to lighten up, April," he said, raising his voice as the conversation escalated. He injected the cat with the medicine and patched it up.

"Why? Why do you not listen to me?" April stuffed the cat back in the cage.

"Because you never get along with anyone. I can plan my calendar around how often I get calls from the school. And yet you wonder why I don't listen to you."

"Maybe if you didn't get butt-hurt over stupid stuff and showed me a little more respect, I'd get along better."

Mr. Day grabbed another cat and handed it to her.

"Respect is something that you have to earn, April. You can't go around treating people the way you do and expect to be treated nicely."

April pinned the cat on the table as they repeated this process.

"What about everyone else? Shouldn't they have to earn my respect, too?"

"Not many people are as rude as you say they are, April. The world isn't like that."

"Maybe if you went outside once in while, instead of staying cooped up in this bunker of a pet hospital, you'd see that I'm right."

"That's uncalled for," Mr. Day shouted.

"It *was* called for. Most people are assholes—especially you. It's no wonder she left you."

Mr. Day fell silent and had a furious look on his face as he continued to administer medication.

"April, get out," he said softly and took the cat away.

"What?" April asked, not sure what he meant.

"April, go home now and don't bother coming in for work tomorrow."

April glared at him. "See what'd I tell you? You're an asshole." With that she stormed out of the room and made her way out of the building.

Not too long after, April boarded the city bus. She deposited her fee and went to the back of the bus. Happy to see that the back was completely vacant, she sat down and fumed over her recent argument.

She reasoned to herself about the futility of her situation. "Why do I have to put up with all this? I'm an epileptic, an adopted child, surrounded by morons, and my reputation is worse thanks to that stupid carnival. Why was I even born?"

She spent the rest of her ride in silence. Finally, the bus stopped at the library. April grabbed her things and exited the bus to find Peggie and Zack waiting for her outside the library.

Peggie was wearing a light blue denim vest over a T-shirt, light blue shorts, and fingerless gloves to match. Zack was wearing a similar outfit in black. As the bus pulled away, a thick black cloud from the exhaust made the three want to gag.

"You guys are already dressed? So we're really doing this then?" April asked.

Peggie looked to the ground and sighed. "Do we really have a choice?"

After a quick glance around the bus stop, April asked, "Where's Jane?"

"Dodie was here not too long ago. She said she needed Jane's help to get the antidote working," Zack said, quickly recapping with a hint of concern in his voice.

"That weird girl again? Isn't she working with the carnival though? Why the heck is she helping us?" April asked.

"I don't know. I'm hoping she doesn't pull a fast one on us," Zack said, bewildered as to what Dodie's intentions were.

"Yeah, I hope Jane will be okay," said Peggie. "I wish she didn't have to go because I have no idea how we're going to do this." The thought of going up against Mimi frightened her.

Zack tried to encourage her. "We're more prepared now. I … I'm sure if we do everything we can, we'll come out all right."

April rolled her eyes. "Way to sound convincing," she said sarcastically.

Zack glared at her. "Why don't you just hurry up and get dressed?"

"Fine, fine," she replied. She walked toward the stone steps of the library, leaving Peggie and Zack alone. Peggie nervously glanced at the football stadium right across the street.

Many cars were beginning to pull into the parking lot, making it look as if a multicolored maze stood between them as well. Peggie sat down on the bench and tried her hardest to convince herself that none of it was real. Try as she might, she was still waiting at the bus stop. She was still waiting for April to get dressed so they might try to convince Mimi to stop her ridiculous plan. But Peggie had a sinking feeling that it wouldn't be possible.

"Hey, we can do this. We got away last time all right," Zack said.

"But we're not running away this time. We might actually have to stay and … and fight her," said Peggie.

"There's three of us. If we can just make sure her henchmen aren't in the way, we'll have the advantage," Zack said again, but was finding Peggie's pessimism hard to break through.

She said, "Didn't you see last time what she can do? She's not like any of the freaks we've seen. She's ... she's strong ... *very* strong." Her eyes welled up with fear.

Zack took a moment to think on this. "You don't have to do this if you don't want to. April and I will still go. We'll find a way to stop the carnival. So ... why don't you just go home?"

Peggie reflected on the offer. It was tempting; why *wouldn't* someone bail? Someone else could do it. It didn't have to be her responsibility. But she came to the dismal conclusion that it was too late. For whatever reason, Janette seemed to have taken an interest in Peggie. Given what had happened with her mother, it was obvious Janette had no self-control and would do anything to mess with her.

"I can't let it go," she said regretfully. "I have to make sure the carnival goes away. I can't leave, not after what happened to Mom. I ... I'm not sure I ever had a chance to get out to begin with." She was trying her best to hide her frustration, but it was written clearly on her face.

Before Zack could comfort her, April arrived in her red version of the same outfit.

"Okay, I'm here. Are we ready to do this?" she asked in a rude tone, doing her best to put on her tough act.

"I am, at least," Zack replied. He looked at Peggie, waiting for her decision. All eyes fell on her, but even without peer pressure the choice was clear.

She took a deep breath and said, "I'm ready." Peggie and Zack stood up, and the three of them gazed at the football stadium. The knowledge that Mimi was in there made the stadium as intimidating as a fortress. Despite their desire and countless opportunities to leave, they went onward into the labyrinth of cars.

A mob swarmed the main entrance to the stadium. The crowd was loud and filling the air with pleas to be let in early to get the best seats. At the head of the crowd was one of Mimi's bouncers, blocking the entrance with his arms folded and an intimidating glare. Or it *would* have been intimidating if it weren't for the clown makeup.

Peggie and her friends remained hidden behind the cars, surveying the area. "Not getting through the front," Zack said quietly.

"No doubt the back will be guarded, too," April added pessimistically.

"But if one of them is here, doesn't that mean the other one is alone?" Peggie asked, trying to approach this strategically.

"So let's take the back one out and go for it," April urged, taking off. The others followed cautiously. The three of them made their way around the stadium and were pleasantly surprised to see the other bouncer guarding the metal doors alone. The three of them remained hidden behind the wall while they examined the area.

"Okay, if we get through this guy, it's a clear shot to Mimi," Zack restated to encourage everyone. Suddenly something occurred to Peggie, and she grabbed Zack and April's arms to keep them from leaving.

"What are you doing?" April said as quietly as she could.

"Wait; maybe we shouldn't rush," Peggie suggested, which earned her confused looks.

"Why shouldn't we?" April asked.

"Well ... if we go after Mimi right away, won't her thugs jump in to help her? Mimi is really strong, right? It's bad enough that we might have to fight *her*. I don't like the idea of having to deal with her henchmen too." Zack and April pondered this silently.

Zack finally admitted: "That's actually a good point."

"So ... what do you want us to do then?" April asked since she was at a loss.

"I was thinking that ... maybe we can lure the other one over. That way we can ambush him, too."

"That could work, but how are we going to do it?" Zack asked. Peggie fell silent.

"Easy," said April. "They're obsessed with Mimi, right? Just bad-mouth her in front of the guy and run, leading him here."

"Yeah, that makes sense," Zack said. "With that kind of logic I'm sure all the fans will keep Mimi distracted."

The three of them quickly went over their strategy and assigned roles to themselves. After double checking to make sure they were all on the same page, April bravely emerged from hiding. With a nonchalant walk, she approached the freak with every intention of being seen.

"Hey! What are you doing here?" the freak snapped. He folded his arms to look more menacing.

"Why, I'm here to ruin Mimi's show. Got a problem with that?" April taunted.

The freak stepped forward. "I know you. You're the brat who punched me before." April began to walk backward, and the freak followed.

"Yeah, and I can do it again if you want," she said, challenging the freak to come at her.

"Don't make light of me, girl. I'm Mimi's top henchman. That makes me something else," he said, gloating and flexing his arms.

"Apparently Mimi sucks then, because you're not impressive at all," April said, continuing to taunt him. Peggie signaled her to stop moving.

"*No one* can talk that way about Mimi. *No one!*" the enraged freak said. He pulled back his fist but was distracted by yelling from the other freak bouncer.

"I'll rip out that tongue of yours, boy!" an enraged, bellowing voice boomed. Zack ran out from behind the corner as Peggie froze the ground with an icy blast.

Zack stopped to make sure he was being followed. When the raging freak charged at him, Zack stepped aside. The freak slipped, fell onto his back, and slid right into the freak threatening April. The second freak fell on top of the first one, pinning him to the ground, leaving the freak on top of the pile stunned and bewildered.

"Now!" Zack signaled. The air around his hands crackled and popped, his hands lit up, and a bolt of lightning spewed forth with a blast. The two freaks twitched uncontrollably, and to add to the pain, April and Peggie began attacking, spewing flames and icy mist into the pile of freaks.

The two freaks disappeared behind the veil of icy mist and blazing flames.

"Tell Mimi I loved her," one of the freaks said.

"Tell Mimi I loved her more," the other freak babbled. The sound of TV static remained.

This alerted the three to stop their attacks, and they watched in awe as the silhouettes composed of a mass of white, black, and gray dots changed shape and shrank.

The blaring sound of TV static died down, and two average men in their late twenties emerged from the silhouettes.

"Good job, team, we did it," Zack said, complimenting the others.

"They weren't really all that bad for freaks," Peggie commented.

"I imagine it'd be nice to feel that way about a girl, but only if she actually loved the guy back. Bit of a shame actually," Zack replied.

"Let's go then. Mimi isn't going to beat herself up," April urged them to follow her to the door. With a bit of focus, April used magic to unlock the door, and the three of them went inside the stadium.

CHAPTER 16

A Full House

M EANWHILE, AS the sun was on the verge of setting, Mimi stared at a large stage built just for her. It was placed right in the center where she could be seen by all. The stage had a large, flat screen towering above it. Lights were stationed in the four corners of the stage, and the microphone stood tall.

Mimi looked around the stadium, taking in the thousands of seats waiting to be filled. She could hear the crowd cheering for her, partly because some of them were already cheering from outside the stadium.

The cool wind blew as Mimi looked up at the cloud-covered sky. "If this is a dream, please don't let it end," she muttered to herself as she closed her eyes and spread out her arms as if basking in her soon-to-be triumph.

"You all set?" Janette asked, smiling wryly from where she sat at the edge of the stage. Mimi jumped from Janette's sudden, unexplained appearance, but immediately put on her signature sunglasses and began to act nonchalantly.

"Of course I am. I am a professional," Mimi said.

Janette leaned back as she lightly swung her feet, which were hanging over the edge, and said, "So it's a big day for you then?"

Mimi took a step toward the bleachers as she gazed up at the soon-to-be-filled seats.

"It is," she replied.

Janette jumped down from the stage and approached emotional Mimi. "A day to never forget?"

Mimi removed her glasses, her eyes welling up with joy. "Yes. I couldn't have done this without you. I wanted to tell you that. Thank you ... thank you so much." Mimi took a deep breath and looked down at her feet, trying to remain calm while Janette stood there, smiling wryly at the situation.

"You're ... you're a good friend," Mimi squeaked, trying hard not to ruin her makeup.

"You're going to do just fine out there. I just built you the stage. The rest is going to be *all* you." Janette smirked as Mimi hugged her tightly.

Mimi looked back at the bleachers and couldn't help but bounce a little with excitement. "Mimi!" voices cried out as people began to fill the bleachers. Mimi and Janette were both surprised by this sudden development.

"Mimi! Mimi! Over here," someone called out to get her attention while waving frantically. The bleachers were quickly filling up. Trigger happy fans flashed their cameras, giddy to be within fifty feet of their idol.

Mimi covered her mouth. She couldn't believe how early they were, but she didn't mind. At last, after all this time, she was going to make her debut to the fans that love her. This was the day that would change everything for her. No more would she have to worry about rejection. No more would she have to worry about being alone. No more would she have to worry about her future.

"Weren't your bodyguards supposed to keep them out?" Janette asked.

"It's fine. I should have known their adoration for me was too much for them. After all ... they're my fans!" Mimi squealed, clapping her hands with excitement.

"I think I'm going to go meet some of them," Mimi giddily informed Janette, then took off to get closer to the bleachers.

Mimi waved to her fans, who filled the stadium with a deafening cheer: "Mimi! Mimi!" Several members of the crowd chanted. Some took the opportunity to take off their shirts to show they had letters of her name painted on their chests. Mimi blushed and laughed a bit at the sight of this silliness.

"Mimi!" a fan right above her called. "Can I have your autograph?" he asked and shoved a concert flyer in front of her face. Before she could accept, another fan got upset.

"No, she's signing mine first!" The jealous fan shoved the eager fan out of the way.

"Hey, I asked her first," the eager fan shouted at him.

"I can give you both autographs," Mimi said, trying to reason with them, but it was futile. The fans had already started a childish argument.

"You don't have as much merchandise as I do; you're not a real fan," the jealous fan said as if the lack of merchandise was somehow proof.

"You don't know what I have," the eager fan countered.

"I bet you don't even like her," the jealous one said again.

"Yes, I do," the eager one insisted.

"Oh yeah? Name one thing you like about her," the jealous one said in challenge.

"Well ... er ... umm ... she's pretty," the eager fan answered unsurely.

This detail caught Mimi's attention. Her face was no longer beaming with a smile. Instead her face was filled with confusion.

"What do *you* like about her?" the eager fan said to return the question.

"I like ... I like ... I *like* her, that's all you need to know," the jealous fan said, grumbling. Mimi's jaw dropped as she began to realize what has happening.

"D-don't any of you like my singing?" she interrupted to ask.

"If you want us to, we will," the jealous fan eagerly replied.

"As long as we get to see you, Mimi, I don't care what you do," the eager fan said, attempting to flatter her. She looked down at the ground as her heart sank.

"Oh … I see … okay then," Mimi mumbled. She solemnly walked away while the fans were calling out to her. It didn't matter that she didn't give them autographs. They wouldn't have meant anything anyway.

She made her way to the locker room. She entered through the doorway and went deeper into the room. She nearly bumped into one of the lockers. The tiled floor had her attention. She walked over to the locker where she kept her makeup.

Inside the locker door was a mirror. She stared into this mirror and was surprised by what she saw. The beautiful soon-to-be pop star, adored by all, was no longer there—or rather never was there. Instead she saw a delusional, untalented, and unwanted woman who had no reason to bother existing. This woman staring back at her was hateful, and she had seemed to despise being in the same room as Mimi.

Mimi's stomach began to sing a familiar tune. An invisible searing knife jabbed into her stomach cavity. The medicine had worn off, and the fatigue she was hiding began to surface again. She hunched over and gasped as the pain punched through her body. Her legs, which felt like they were made of noodles, collapsed, and her head banged against the lockers as she fell.

She winced in pain as she slowly pulled herself up to reach into her locker. Her hand felt around for her bag. Finally finding it, Mimi clenched the strap in her fist and allowed gravity to take her once more. The bag fell to the floor next to her. She crouched over with her stomach threatening to rip itself in half if she didn't pay attention to it.

Mimi frantically took out a bottle of white pills and gulped down what must've been a handful of pills—enough to overdose a normal person. With the help of a water bottle that she had packed for this occasion, she ingested the medicine. Instinctively, she grabbed an energy bar and began to munch down on it. However, she stopped herself halfway and observed what she had eaten.

This is all I've got going for me? she thought to herself. She chucked the energy bar across the room to prevent herself from eating any more in fear of ruining her figure.

"I just … I just need to sing is all. They'll like me for that," she said to herself. It was difficult to believe in this lie, though, in view of the behavior she observed from her "adoring" fans. Would they even care for her song? Would they even acknowledge it as long as they are brainwashed by her poison? Even then, how would she know if they actually like listening to her sing or are doing just because she wants them to? The only thing she knew now was that they just wanted to see her but not listen.

Mimi took a few moments to calm herself. She still hadn't fully regained her composure, but the pain subsided, and her weakness was once again hidden from the world. Her concert should have started two minutes ago. There was no more time to rest: She had to go out there and put on a show. She had come so far with this strategy to get noticed, and she couldn't turn back now.

With that Mimi got up off the floor and left the locker room. She entered the hallway and walked toward the field. The moment she stepped into the light, she immediately heard the cheering of her many, many fans. Nearly half the stadium was filled. With future concerts her fans would be widespread enough to fill the entire stadium. So as not to disappoint, Mimi made the most out of this moment by waving toward everyone and even blowing a few kisses as she traversed the field.

Mimi climbed the steps to her stage and stood before the microphone, giddy with excitement until some fans screamed: "We love you Mimi!" This provoked a sharp pain in Mimi's heart, and she hesitated to speak into the microphone.

Eventually the fans quieted down, waiting eagerly for her to start the show. She took a deep breath, grasped the microphone, and removed it from the stand. "Thank you all for coming tonight," she said. A few fans whistled in response to finally hearing her voice.

"You all ready to have some fun?" she asked, egging on the crowd that responded with a bellowing yes. Mimi smiled. The enthusiasm was music to her ears. She was finally going to fulfill her dream of performing in front of a live audience. Mimi cleared her throat when the speakers started playing music.

Mimi counted the beats, getting into the tempo of her song. But just as she was about to sing, a bolt of electricity suddenly struck the screen hanging overhead. The screen shattered, and pieces of glass fell to the ground, leaving a smoking hole where the image used to be.

"Now what?" Mimi complained and stamped her foot, seeing that her concert had been interrupted yet again. In a moment the lights came back on and illuminated the area.

"Mimi!" Zack yelled out to her. Mimi looked around and saw the three would-be heroes emerge from the locker rooms.

"Ugh, you again?" Mimi growled. "Haven't you've done enough already?"

"Obviously not," April replied with a similar tone of voice.

Peggie looked Mimi straight in the eye. "Mimi!" she called out.

"What do you want?" Mimi snapped.

Peggie huffed and said: "I want you to leave. Leave my city—*now!*"

Upon hearing this, Mimi threw a fit. "Are you people jealous of me or something? What have I ever done to you?"

Peggie was furious at this accusation, "No, I'm not jealous. I want you out of my city. You hurt my Mom. Now I want you gone."

"So what if she got hurt? I needed her out of the way. How else am I supposed to get noticed in this shit hole of a city? Just go away and leave me alone. I just want to sing."

Mimi cried while having an emotional meltdown on stage.

"Whoa, she's lost it," Zack commented, pointing out the obvious.

But Peggie was a bit confused by Mimi's behavior. *Is she ... crying?* Peggie asked herself. Mimi now appeared more like someone who was desperate than evil.

"Boys!" Mimi shouted, trying to summon her personal bodyguards.

Mimi looked around, puzzled by their absence. "Boys, get rid of them! Where are you, damn it?"

"They can't help you," Zack said. "We've already cured them. Now leave the city's water alone or else!" He was confident they had the advantage.

Mimi's eyes widened at this ludicrous demand, "No! Why? *Every ... single ... time ...* it turns out this way!"

"What are you kids doing?" "Get off the field!" "Can't you see she's doing a show?" Voices from the crowd raged. One person smacked April in the head with an empty soda can.

"Throw that again, I dare you," April threatened, baring her teeth like a wild animal.

"Focus on Mimi. It's not their fault," Zack said. He ducked from the onslaught of trash being thrown at them. The three of them put distance between themselves and the audience.

April gave Mimi two choices. "All right, so what's it going to be? Are you going to stop, or do we need to smack you?"

This was the final push that put Mimi over the edge.

"No! No, I don't want to. I'm going to get noticed. I'm going to have this concert one way or the other," she said, shrieking and stamping her foot on the stage.

This must have been some sort of signal: Hidden compartments on the stage opened up and shot out hot air balloons that quickly filled up with heat from roaring flames.

CHAPTER 17

The Marvelous Mimi

THE THREE heroes could barely believe the sight before them. Mimi's stage began to wobble when the giant traffic-cone-orange hot air balloons rose into the sky and lifted the stage off the ground. But Mimi was determined—no, *desperate*—to present this "concert."

April was stunned at the sight. "Is she serious?" Her question was answered shortly when Peggie and Zack sprinted toward the stage, prompting April to follow suit. When the stage began to lift off the ground, the three of them desperately jumped onto it. Zack and April managed to pull themselves up on the stage, but Peggie hung from some of the bars below.

Mimi was furious at their persistent determination to ruin her show. "Get off *my* stage!" she screeched and rushed over to their side.

"You help Peggie," April ordered Zack and quickly got between him and Mimi.

April threw a punch at Mimi, who simply grabbed April's arm and threw her against the furthest speaker. The speaker fell off the edge and fell to the ground, smashing to smithereens.

Just as Zack was pulling Peggie up, the stage began to tilt. Mimi tried desperately to keep her balance as she slid toward the edge. Zack lost his grip on Peggie, and he slid toward the edge of the stage, forcing Peggie to grab the bar once again.

The stage soon became so lopsided as it continued to ascend that they all had to hang onto whatever they could find. The stage began to float toward the end of the stadium, its foolish passengers holding on for dear life. Peggie looked down and saw they were nearing the height of the stadium lights while everyone below watched in awe, making no attempts to call for help.

Mimi panicked at seeing her dangling feet when they passed over the bleachers. "No! My glasses," she shrieked when her fashionable accessory fell on some lucky person's head.

Peggie's heart pounded as she looked for a way down, finding nothing safe to catch her fall. When she looked up at the balloons, it dawned on her that they were the answer. With every bit of courage she could muster, she took one hand off the bar and conjured up long, thin icicles that floated around her hand. She aimed her hand carefully as the icicles hovered in the cloud of mist emitted from her hand, took a deep breath, and with one motion launched the icicles. They pierced the balloons, causing them to lose air. The stage began to move past the stadium much faster until they hovered over the parking lot and began to descend quickly to the pavement.

"Jump!" Zack yelled.

"What? Are you nuts?" Peggie shrieked.

"We have armor, it'll hurt more if we crash."

"We're dead anyway. Let's do it," April said in agreement and let go.

"April!" Peggie screamed as if it would reverse her decision.

April landed on the roof of a car, leaving a large dent with her feet when she collided. "Hurry up!" she shouted when they were only a few feet above the ground. Peggie closed her eyes when she and Zack let go.

The two landed on their feet and tumbled over. Seconds later the sound of metal banging and bending sounded when the stage crashed into the ground and crumbled into a trash heap.

April leaped from atop the car and joined her two friends, who looked in awe at the dismantled stage. When Mimi gazed at the pile, her tears welled up once more. She covered her mouth and turned away from the mess, her dreams once again crushed by the people that constantly surrounded her. She began to question the world. "Why? Every single time! Why?"

Mimi glared with rage at the three heroes. Her face turned as red as an apple from fuming over this development. She faced the nearest vehicle, which happened to be a large truck, and with all of her strength lifted it off the ground and held it over her head.

"Geez!" Zack said, emitting a startled cry.

"You three are *dead!*" Mimi screamed. With the full weight of her body, she threw the truck at them. Her opponents had expected this and were already moving out of the way when the truck zoomed past them, hit the ground, flipped over, skidded across the cement, and bumped into the stadium wall, which crushed its bumper.

The three heroes exchanged glances, all of them having second thoughts about confronting this Amazonian woman. Peggie looked up and saw Mimi charging at her. Peggie scrambled to her feet, but Mimi caught and lifted her off the ground by her shirt. She pulled back a fist, ready to punch her into the air. Peggie screamed as she held out her hands and doused Mimi in thick, freezing, white mist.

The sudden burst of cold startled Mimi, and she dropped Peggie onto the floor. "Peggie, stay down!" April ordered, running at Mimi with her flaming fists. April landed a punch in Mimi's stomach. The flames burst into a small explosion. Mimi flew back and landed hard on the ground, cradling her stomach.

April helped Peggie up, while Mimi painfully tried to get up herself. Zack blasted Mimi further back with bolts of lightning, pushing the superpowered villainess against a car. Mimi slowly got up despite still being zapped.

"I guess lightning doesn't work on her," he muttered, beginning to feel useless.

"Let me help," Peggie offered. She blasted Mimi with a stream of cold mist. April joined in as well, spewing a pillar of fire from her hands.

Mimi was pushed to the ground, but soon she regained her footing and rose to fight against their combined force.

April groaned. "Why isn't it working?" Mimi began to block the streams of magic with her arms and charged at them.

The three of them immediately bailed as Mimi rushed past them. "She must be too strong," Peggie pessimistically concluded.

"Then how did I hit her so hard?" April asked, confused by this sudden inconsistency.

Mimi lifted her leg and with a mighty stomp jammed her high heel into the pavement. As if there had been an earthquake, the pavement began to crack and split. The three heroes instinctively ran away from the ominously orange glowing crack that zipped toward them.

The glowing crack made a hard turn and homed in on them. The three found themselves blockaded by the parked cars. They hadn't anticipated this strange attack would chase them. The crack went right under their feet and then sprawled out like a glowing spider as its glow intensified. The three sprinted away from this web just in time to avoid a geyser of concrete and fire. Nearby cars went airborne and flipped over a lane of cars before crashing to the ground.

April and Zack were baffled by this absurd sight. Peggie nervously looked at Mimi, wondering what she would do next. It was then she noticed that Mimi had her hand over stomach and was crouched over. An indication of stomach pain perhaps? If so, they'd be crazy not to exploit it. Peggie called April, regaining the attention of her friends.

"Hit her stomach again! Hit like really hard, as much as you can," Peggie said. Of course, Mimi didn't like this idea, so she stomped her foot on the ground, causing cracks to spread out in all directions.

Peggie and Zack frantically tried to escape, but April grabbed hold of her friends' arms, keeping them still.

"What, are you crazy?" Zack asked. The explosive cracks all homed in on their position. April waited for all the cracks to converge under them.

April then pulled her two friends along just as the ground beneath them became a mass of cracks. A fiery geyser erupted from that spot, heating the air around them. A large hole was left where they stood moments ago. April's heart pounded as the gush of air and heat brushed against her neck. Peggie and Zack were surprised at April's stroke of genius.

But Mimi was prepared for this. She slammed her fist into the ground with all her might, creating a shock wave that knocked the three off their feet and sent them flying into the cars nearby. Peggie slammed into a windshield, crashing through it and into the passenger seat. The force of her collision was enough to make the car stand up on its rear bumper and slowly topple backward. Peggie tumbled around in the back seat of the car, screaming as it cashed loudly. The top of the car crumpled like paper, trapping Peggie inside. Her face and legs were cut by the glass that fell on her.

Zack was thrown into a street light. He crashed through it and snapped the pole in two. The light crashed into the ground, scattering glass all over the pavement. Zack skidded and tumbled into the hood of a car. April rocketed into the side of a car with force so tremendous that the entire row of cars slid over several spaces before April's body detached itself from the unusable car door. She slinked to the ground, confused and shocked by what she just experienced.

The three of them winced in pain as red-faced Mimi marched toward Peggie. She tried to get out, but the twisted window was too small. Mimi grabbed the car door, yanked it clear off its hinges, and tossed it aside with a loud thud. Peggie tried to kick Mimi away, but Mimi grabbed her foot, dragged her out of her vehicular prison, and lifted Peggie by her shirt with a death grip. Mimi was about to punch Peggie in the face, but while she dangled there, Peggie formed a thick ball of ice in her hand. A punch of that magnitude would go straight through her skull.

Mimi twitched when Zack zapped her with a bolt of electricity. Peggie saw this opening. She concentrated hard to get a few extra layers of ice on the ball and fired it as hard as she could at Mimi's stomach. The ice ball shattered and some of its shrapnel pelted Peggie, leaving additional minor cuts on her body.

Mimi staggered back, wincing in pain and holding her stomach. Peggie's heart pounded and she couldn't stop. Moved by adrenaline, she got on her feet and prepared another sphere.

Mimi shielded her stomach in anticipation, but Peggie fired a cold mist from her hand right into Mimi's face to stagger her then fired the sphere at her stomach again. Mimi stumbled backward and fell on her rear as she collapsed from the pain.

Zack and April were awed by how well Peggie was doing. But Peggie was trembling. She was defending herself well but was nearing her mental limits and could barely keep herself standing.

April and Zack got on their feet and approached Peggie but were stopped by Mimi's final act of desperation. Mimi's became enveloped by purple smoke that violently fumed from her body. The three of them stepped away from Mimi, unsure what this meant.

When Mimi waved her hand, a clump of purple smoke shot out from her hand into the air and formed a ringlike cloud. Then it began to rain ... it rained *speakers* that landed with a loud thud. They stacked on top of each other. With each passing second, the four sorcerers found themselves increasingly trapped in a room with walls that grew higher and higher. The walls reached two stories before the odd storm ended. Mimi was seething with anger, grunting and moaning, trying to get up. A headset emerged from the smoke and appeared on Mimi, who glared at her three adversaries with contempt.

Her three opponents were caught completely off guard by this. Mimi twisted a dial in her headset, and a short sound burst from the speakers signifying that they were turned on to the highest possible volume.

"Crap!" April said with a gasp. She ignited her fist and dashed madly dash toward Mimi, but too late to act.

At first there was a high-pitched scream. Then for the three heroes everything fell silent as their vision blurred and they lost all feeling in their bodies. Even with blurred vision, they knew they had fallen to the ground. The numbness they felt was as if every nerve in their bodies vibrated—as if tiny jackhammers had invaded their insides. The battle armor the three heroes wore had begun to glow violently.

After what must have been ten or fifteen seconds of screaming, Mimi ran out of breath. The speakers dissolved into clouds of smoke and faded away. The glow of the armor faded, and the loud sound of tearing could be heard. The vests that they had worn had been decimated and were barely being held together by the handful of strands that didn't break.

The three heroes' vision gradually returned. So did the feeling of pain: They ached all over. Meanwhile, Mimi trembled and breathed heavily from the ordeal she had just endured. Her rage was leaving her. Only exhaustion remained. The combatants were too worn out to move, so finally they took a moment to rest.

CHAPTER 18

Final Performance

"**G**OOD JOB, Mimi, you sure showed them," a familiar voice said along with a series of claps. Mimi looked around and saw Janette slowly approach the tuckered-out superstar.

"I did … I did, didn't I?" She smiled in between pants, proud of dealing with the party crashers. Janette examined Mimi very closely and in an obviously insincere voice, said: "Oh Mimi, are you okay? Are you hurt anywhere?"

Mimi took Janette's hand as she was helped up. "No, I just … need to catch my breath." Janette looked around at the downed heroes, who were too exhausted to get up.

"We can still do the show you, know," Janette said with a mischievous smile.

"We can?" Mimi brightened up and stared at Janette with big, gleaming eyes full of hope.

"Sure we can. I had a backup plan," Janette said, reassuring her. She pulled out a video recorder, a microphone, a director's chair, and a small stereo from her hat. "There's this thing called the Internet. With some special effects, I'm sure your video will go viral. Everyone would talk about you for months."

Mimi brightened up, "You can't get any bigger than the Internet! Thank you! Thank you, Janette! You always come through for me." Janette smiled queerly and handed her the microphone.

"Of course. We're friends, after all," Janette replied smugly.

Mimi brushed herself off, did some vocal exercises, then waited impatiently with a beaming smile. Janette flipped the screen open on the side of the recorder and removed the lens cap.

"Ready?" Janette asked. Mimi nodded, fidgeting with so much excitement that you'd never realize she was just in a fight.

"We're like right here still. What are they doing?" April asked.

"Being ridiculous." Zack muttered.

Mimi looked back at them and yelled vehemently, "Quiet! You will *not* take this from me."

Janette gave a friendly smile to Mimi. "Don't worry. If they try anything, they'll get a dagger in the face—a very *hot* dagger," she threatened with bloodlust in her voice.

Feeling reassured, Mimi gave the go-ahead. "Okay, I'm ready."

"Lights! Camera! Action!" Janette announced as the recorder's red light of turned on. "Hello Internet! It's me, your favorite celebrity, Mimi!" she said to introduce herself.

"I'm going to give you all quite a show tonight. Even Beverly Fame will be blown out of the water by this performance. Are you ready? Three, two, one!" Mimi said into the microphone before finally starting her song.

Music started playing from the speaker under the chair, and Mimi began singing.

Don't you know I'm hotter than the summer sun?

Say you love me, hey, hey!

Don't you know I'm cooler than the winter breeze?

Say you love me!

I know you all wish you were me,

but that is just a fantasy.

Mimi was really into her song at this point, and it was on this line that Janette's plan was revealed.

In a puff of smoke, a metal bucket appeared over Mimi's head. The bucket turned over and poured pig slop all over the not-so-innocent singer. Mimi screamed, as she even got some of the warm, wet combination of spoiled food into her mouth.

When the bucket fell and hit Mimi in the head, the speaker began to play prerecorded sounds of an audience giggling and laughing. Janette burst into an unnatural fit of laughter.

Mimi was freaking out as she spat the slop out of her mouth and began to scream and cry. Mimi stared at Janette, who was hunched over, holding her sides in a hysterical fit of laughter.

"Wh ... Why? Why did ... why did you do that?" Mimi squeaked, in a quivering voice and on the verge of hysteria.

"Because it's funny," Janette taunted. Mimi was speechless as she tried to process this sudden turn of events.

She tried to speak. "I ... I thought you were my ..."

"What? your friend?" Janette replied spitefully. "You mean the one whose place you thought you could take in the show? The one who you left? The one you abandoned after all I've done for you? Ah-ha-ha! You're getting what you deserve!"

Mimi recalled the event and finally realized what happened. "Was it ... was it you who gave me that microphone?"

Janette replied, "Of course. Did you think you could rub me out of the show? I pulled a little prank on you to get you back in line, but *no*—you had to go and leave me, even when you knew that no one wants to listen to a *fat cow* sing. How dare you think I wouldn't be pissed!"

"But ... but they *do!*" Mimi insisted and fell to her knees.

Janette looked down on her and replied, "No they don't, and you know why." Janette looked around at the three heroes, who were speechless.

"I had my revenge. I hope you're looking forward to that Internet video." Janette bid Mimi farewell and began to fly off but stopped to throw in one final remark.

"Oh, and Peggie: I sure hope your Mom is enjoying her new tan. I'm sure she'll turn a few heads now … *away!*" Janette laughed childishly at her own joke. Peggie clenched her fist. The desire to punch her in the face was overwhelming. Janette, having accomplished her mission of spreading misery, flew off into the night.

Mimi was left to sob while the three heroes regained the strength to move. Peggie had a sharp pain in her back and had to use the nearest car to pull herself up.

At that point, Jane finally arrived on the scene.

"Oh my gosh, are you okay? Look, I can distract her while you guys run," Jane suggested, noticing their armor was damaged.

Peggie looked at the smooth white silhouette of her friend and replied, "N-no, it's okay. I don't think she'll hurt anyone anymore." Poor, depressed Mimi had curled into a ball, buried her face in her knees, and was crying her eyes out.

Jane expressed her relief. "So she's been subdued? That's good."

"Yeah, but just barely," Peggie said. "We would have died without this armor. So what about the water? Did Dodie fix it like she said?"

Jane was hesitant, "Yes she did. In a few days, no one will be obsessed with Mimi."

Peggie found this behavior odd but pushed it out of her mind when Zack and April approached to join the conversation.

"Good! Having to drink bottled water is expensive," said Zack, groaning as he limped toward the two girls. His leg had already formed a large black bruise that stung with each step he took.

April clutched her arm. "Terrific. Now what are going to do about her?" She motioned toward the wailing superstar.

Peggie stared at her feet, contemplating events up till now. "It appears that Mimi wasn't doing all of this just to hurt people. If she wanted to do that, she had plenty of opportunity. Also, Janette just humiliated her. If anything, Mimi was just the victim of something else getting out of hand. If so, then maybe …" She gazed at pitiful Mimi and said, "I'm going to talk with her." Zack and April were astounded.

"Peggie, that's crazy. She's evil," Zack said.

"Do you have a death wish? Talking won't do anything," said April.

"I know. Everyone from the carnival is crazy, but …" Peggie said.

Zack interrupted. "You're not going to do it. Don't be stupid! We'll just find a way to lock her up or something."

April was happy to share her own idea. "No, that's dumb. We should just kill her. That way we'll never have to worry about her."

Naturally, Zack opposed this idea and tried to get Jane on his side. "You can find a way to lock her up, right?"

Jane was surprised by her sudden involvement. "I can think of something, but I'm not sure it would hold her."

"See? Then kill her!" April repeated, thinking her approach was the most sensible.

"She hasn't killed anyone herself," Zack said.

"And how the shit would you know if she did or not? You've seen her: She's crazy. If she hasn't killed yet, she will."

"You can say that about anyone," Zack fired back, trying to exploit a loophole.

"Okay, you tell me how a ghost, who had to get our help just to confront her, is supposed to lock her up? There is no way in hell that any prison is going to stop her."

Meanwhile, Peggie had already gone to Mimi's side.

Zack said, "Peggie is with me on this. Right? Peggie? Peggie, what are you doing? Get back here!" He was afraid she'd get her head torn off. Peggie was terrified of this thought, too, but she figured Mimi was too distraught to do such a thing, so she ignored Zack. Despite her earlier beliefs, it was clear that Mimi was a victim of the carnival, too.

Maybe if I talk to her now she'll go away on her own, Peggie thought. She hesitantly knelt beside Mimi. She groaned with each inch that she lowered herself.

"Um ..." Peggie began, searching for the right words to say.

"Go away!" Mimi cried, turning away when she noticed Peggie.

"Is there anything I can do to help?" Peggie asked, sympathizing with the woman.

"No. I won't be lied to again. You're just here to make fun of me. All of you are." Mimi screamed at the air and continued to sob. Her tears were washing the bits of beans and ketchup that clung to her face, forming a puke-colored puddle on the ground.

"I try so hard to look the way everyone wants me to. They wouldn't even give me the time of day before. Now, after everything I've done, I get treated like this. It's not fair."

"People are assholes. We just have to deal with it," said April, who had walked over to join them.

Mimi shoved her hand into the earth below, pulled out a hand-sized chunk of concrete, and hurled it at April. April screamed as she ducked. The missile tore through the metal of the car behind her.

"How about we just let Peggie deal with this, okay April?" Jane suggested. Meanwhile, a street light further down the parking lot toppled over.

Peggie hesitated to answer. "You know … looks aren't everything."

"Yes they are," Mimi shrieked.

Peggie immediately distanced herself from Mimi, expecting to get punted across the parking lot. However, Mimi just continued her disheartened dialogue.

"I tried out to sing on *USA Idol*. I practiced so much. I sang every day. Singing … singing always cheered me up: on the days when I was home alone, on the days I was picked on, on the days I was humiliated, on the days I was rejected. I sang every day, thinking, 'I'll be a famous singer. Everyone will want to hear me sing.' They'd actually listen to me and hear what I have to say. For the first time, they would actually *see* me."

Peggie couldn't help but empathize with Mimi a little bit. Peggie thought of Mimi as just some crazy person who was obsessed with singing, but now she wasn't so sure. The things Mimi did couldn't be completely forgiven, but she wasn't as big of a monster as Peggie thought.

"I sang so much," Mimi continued. "I practiced every day. I finally worked up the courage to audition, but I still couldn't make the cut. 'People want to feel good about themselves,' and 'We'll never be able to sell any products with a fat girl on the cover,' were things they said, and I realized … they were right. On all the magazines, even on the underwear in stores, you find only beautiful people. No one … no one really wants to advertise fat people."

"Was that really the reason they rejected you?" Peggie asked, shocked by this news.

Mimi looked at her in disbelief. "Of course it was. Have you not been paying attention? All the actors, all the clothes models, the people on TV—they're all people who look good. People want to look good because it makes them feel good. That's why I look like this now, so I could finally be able to sing. So ... so that people would actually *listen* to me ... so that I could feel good for once."

Mimi held her forehead because a headache was coming on. "I thought ... I thought Janette understood. I didn't really care what she did or what kind of person she was. She listened ... she understood. And now ... she does this?" Mimi burst into tears again as the sting of betrayal finally set in.

Peggie held her tongue as she tried to think of what to say next.

"I guess ... you're right about that," she said. "We all want to feel good about ourselves. We keep saying that looks don't matter, but in the end ... I guess they kind of do. We keep worrying about what to wear, or our figures, and other people judge us for it. I did it, too, and I didn't realize it till now. To be honest, sometimes I wish I didn't have to wear glasses. I'm also a bit envious of people who wear contacts. I'm not exactly comfortable sticking my fingers in my eyes. You're completely right: We do care, and we do like to see beautiful people. There's nothing wrong with that until it gets taken too far."

"Then why doesn't anyone want to listen to me?" Mimi asked. "Why aren't I allowed to sing?" Mimi longed for an answer as she stared wearily at Peggie.

"That's because even though looking good is nice, we can't rely on it to be liked. I mean, aren't there a lot of celebrities that people hate, even though they look good?"

Mimi's face was overcome with confusion. "B-but ... what did I do to make them hate me?"

Peggie quietly recalled her previous encounter with Mimi. "You were *forcing* them to like you," she answered as gently as possible since she wanted to keep her head where it was. "Maybe you should try to let people *choose* to listen to your singing. You know ... let your talent do more of the work. No one likes doing anything they don't want to do, and they like the people who force them even less. It's perfectly okay to advertise, but you can't force yourself on people. Anyone who does like your singing will find you, but if you disrespect them, then they won't have anything to do with you."

Mimi looked to the ground as she contemplated this. She finally stood up, and Peggie followed. Mimi clasped her hands together and looked at Peggie in sorrowful desperation.

"I tried to let people listen to me, but that didn't work. What makes you think it'll work now? What's different about it now?" she asked, skeptical of this suggestion.

Peggie gave Mimi a look of pity. "Because I'm here. I will listen to you sing. You can sing as much as you want for me. You just need to promise me something: Stop all of this. Don't poison the water any more. If you do that, you're going to hurt people who don't deserve your anger. There's already so much wrong with this city. Please, Mimi. Please don't add to it."

Mimi's eyes lit up with a glimmer of hope. "I promise," she said, nodding firmly. "That's all I really ever wanted. So ... may I sing now?" she asked, bouncing enthusiastically like a child getting candy.

Peggie smiled warmly. "Go ahead. You've wanted this so badly; I couldn't think of going back on my promise."

Mimi brushed away some of the slop and picked up the microphone. She raised the microphone to her mouth. Street lamp light shone down on her from above in another attempt to put on a show.

The group cringed at the mere thought of hearing Mimi sing. They were well aware of Mimi's style of music: It wasn't good. Mimi cleared her throat and to everyone's surprise started to sing a different song. It was slow, and the lyrics were much less conceited. This time Mimi expressed her pain through the song and attempted to connect to the audience.

A surge of inspiration came to Mimi when a familiar image entered her mind.

> Open your eyes; look at me.
> Won't you see the woman I've grown up to be?
> I want you here, in this place, here with me,
> Like how it was meant to be.
> The people here—they all know;

They're not unique, just more fish in the sea.
This place is filled with fear, so much fear;
That's why I want you here.
Oh please, Mother, won't you please open your eyes?
Before you die, I want you here not there,
In that place, in blissful sleep.
Mother, please come back to me,
To this world, to this place so lonely.
It's been years! Can you hear?
Do my words fall on deaf ears?
Am I not enough? Do I have the stuff?
Oh please, just tell me why; I don't want to say goodbye.
Mother, please look at me! Won't you please listen to me?
Hear my plea, I need you here,
In this place filled with so much fear.
I can't stand it here while you are there.
I want your gaze, I want your praise.
I want to go back to those better days.
I know it's not likely, but mother please hear my plea.
Come back to me ... come back to me.

At the end of this song Mimi wore a solemn expression. Her audience was dumbfounded by the performance. In a few seconds, Mimi snapped back to reality. "Umm ... so how was that?" she asked, feeling tension in her toes and hands as she began fidgeting.

"That ... wasn't bad, actually," Zack admitted, finally feeling safe to approach the wannabe singer.

Mimi's face brightened up as she heard this. "Really?"

At this moment April strolled in. "Eh ... the lyrics could use work, but you actually have a nice voice to listen to. Unless you plan on practicing a whole lot, you might want to let a lyricist make up the songs for you instead. Otherwise people will think you're talking gibberish."

Peggie and Zack looked at April in disbelief. Was she trying to get their heads torn off? Mimi's jaw dropped as she gazed at the three of them.

"You all ... actually think I'm good?" She squeaked from trying to hold back the excitement. Peggie and Zack sighed with relief that Mimi didn't seem to mind the harsh critic.

Peggie smiled. "Yeah, I think it was a pretty nice song. It was a bit sad, though. What made you sing that?"

A large smile stretched across Mimi's face. Her talent was finally being recognized, and she wanted to cry. Her chest was warm from overwhelming happiness.

"I don't know, I sang that. It just ... sorta ..." Mimi's head felt heavy.

Suddenly the strength left Mimi's legs. She fell to her knees and toppled over onto the ground.

"Whoa! Are you all right?" Zack asked as the three of them surrounded her.

Mimi had begun to breathe heavily, and she felt weak and dizzy. Worse, she could barely feel the cold, rough pavement beneath her. "I-I'll... I'll get help," Peggie stuttered and frantically reached for her phone.

"Hey you're going to be okay, right?" Zack asked.

"You happy now?" he said to April.

"I didn't mean it," she said.

Zack focused his attention on Mimi, but April hung back, unsure of what to do because she was feeling guilty. Meanwhile, Mimi's breathing became increasingly irregular, so Zack grabbed hold of her hand to calm her.

"You're going to be all right. Pegs is getting an ambulance. Just hang on."

Mimi smiled softly. "I'm more than all right."

Before Peggie could push the send button on her phone, Mimi began to flicker like a television. Her body was gradually replaced by a flickering silhouette composed of TV static.

Mimi looked up at them all and bid farewell. "Promise me: If you find anyone else like me ... save them, too," she asked, then let out a painful cry as she was completely engulfed by static. The shape of the silhouette distorted, becoming a violent, thrashing blob that knocked Zack back onto his butt. The violent distortions began to settle and form the shape of a person—someone not Mimi.

Everyone stared in awe and surprise. There was only one reason this event would occur. Just as they all realized what it meant, Mimi finished her transformation. In her place was a younger, more portly girl. Mimi's entire existence was almost completely explained by this phenomenon.

They all gathered around to examine the sleeping girl, and Peggie gasped. "Wait ... so does this mean ..."

Jane hovered over this young, dark-haired female. "Mimi wasn't a real person. She was freakified like all the other victims."

April scowled. "What do you mean she wasn't real?"

Jane shook her head. "It was Mimi who did all those things, not this girl. Mimi must've been an alternate personality. Now that the spell is broken ... Mimi is dead."

April hung her head low as a surge guilt washed over her. "I didn't know she was a victim."

"Do you think she'll remember anything?" Zack asked.

"It's hard to say. In some cases, people can remember what happened while they were enchanted. But it depends on the nature of the spell and the person it was cast on."

April suggested: "We could just ask her. She might be able to tell us something. Her transformation was freakishly different from the others."

"That's a good idea," Zack said, agreeing with April for once. "We might even get an advantage if she can tell us any secrets."

Peggie fixated on this new girl with a solemn look on her face. She wasn't sure whether she should mourn for Mimi.

"But what did we do to change her back?" Peggie asked, thinking Mimi would have changed back much sooner during the fight. After all, the normal method was just beating away at the spell with brute force.

Jane thought for a moment and then explained her hypothesis. "Mimi must've been created from this girl's desires. Umm ... to put it simply, you've basically proven that Mimi didn't need to exist any more. To put it simply, Mimi broke the spell by herself."

"So Mimi committed suicide?" April asked.

"This is very weird magic," Jane replied. "There is no way of knowing for sure. What we do know is that Mimi is gone. It's better this way, I think."

"Hey, doesn't she look familiar?" said Zack. Everyone looked at him in surprise.

"You know her?" Jane asked.

"No, she just looks like someone I've seen before."

Peggie and April studied the girl's features closely. Suddenly April's memory came flooding back. "I used to make fun of this girl."

Zack glared sternly at April. "Wouldn't surprise me if she ended up like this because of you." April opened her mouth to defend herself, but she couldn't find the words.

"Sh-shut up!" she retorted.

Before the argument could escalate, Peggie yelped. "It's her. She was the first kid to go missing at our school. You remember her, right Zack? We were talking about it at lunch the day Sal was taken."

Zack took another look at the girl. "Oh geez, you're right. Peggie, call up an ambulance again. April, help me move her!"

"Why move her?" April asked.

"Because the first thing they'll see is this and then they would want answers," Zack replied. He pointed to the nearby trash pile that was once a stage.

While April and Zack painstakingly moved the heavy girl, Peggie summoned an ambulance. They waited impatiently, but finally heard the sirens from a few blocks away. The paramedics arrived, saw the unconscious girl, and whisked her away as quickly as they could.

Even though they were concerned for the girl's well-being, they had no choice but to return home. After all, they were supposed to be studying at the library, and it was already nighttime.

CHAPTER 19

Things to Come

OVER THE weekend, the city began to forget about Mimi. People went about their business as if the young, upcoming "straitjacket sensation" never existed. During that time, the Shadow Carnival was quiet, which in Peggie's book was welcomed because she was able to take the time to visit her Mom in the hospital.

It was a good day to visit the hospital. The sun shone brightly in the sky, and no clouds were in sight. The temperature was just right. A cool breeze was blowing and scattering the colorful leaves of autumn.

Peggie's mother was staring at her cell phone, reading a text message. The opening of the door caught her attention as a pleasant surprise.

"Peggie!" her Mom said cheerfully and opened her arms wide to give her daughter a hug.

"Hi Mom," Peggie said. Crossing the polished tiled floor, she approached to accept her mother's hug but noticed her skin. Patches of red were all over her face, arms, and hands.

Ms. Worth was puzzled by this reaction and then realized her gaze was directed at her wounds.

"I'm fine. Really. Come here," her mother said, beckoning Peggie to come closer. Taking her word for it, Peggie gave her mother a loving hug while trying to hold back her tears. It hurt to see those burn marks embedded on her mother's skin. It was an unwanted reminder of the Shadow Carnival, a reminder of that girl Janette.

Peggie sat down in the chair next to the bed, ready to enjoy some conversation. Her mother immediately fired a barrage of questions: "So how have you been doing? Have you been eating right? Are you doing your homework?"

"I'm doing fine. I cooked all my meals like you showed me, and I'm getting Bs and As in school. So what about you? Have you been doing okay?" Peggie was worried about her mom.

"I'm feeling much better. The doctors here are really nice. They even helped throw a birthday party for one of the patients here. But I don't think I'm going to be buying anything from salesmen anymore," she jokingly replied.

"Right—Please don't, especially if they're wearing a top hat. In fact, how about you stay away from anyone that wears a hat like that?" Peggie stressed, wanting to make sure her Mom knew to stay away if she ever saw Janette again.

"I'm really more worried for you right now. Have you been listening to the news? There's this weird gang that's causing trouble for everyone in the city, dressed up like clowns no less!"

Peggie nodded. "Yeah I know. Some people are getting hurt because of them."

"I want you to come straight home from now on, okay? All the kids have to be home by six now anyway, with the new curfew coming into effect and all."

Peggie was surprised to hear this. "The curfew's being changed? Really?"

Her mother nodded. "Yes, the mayor ruled for a stricter curfew because of all the violence happening lately."

"Oh well, can't really argue with that."

"Still, I doubt he'll get re-elected. I can already tell that woman Dodie Hammers is going to win the election."

Peggie was surprised to hear this name. "*Who* is Dean Narrow running against?"

"Dodie Hammers. From what I've heard, she has a promising background in education and medicine and claims to have plans to fix things."

Peggie was uneasy because she knew only one person named Dodie. "Oh yeah, I think I might've heard of her. Do you know what she looks like?"

"I don't know what she looks like. She hasn't made any public appearances yet. Normally that would be bad for an election, but with Dean so occupied with finding his daughter, anyone would be better. Honestly, there's not a doubt in my mind he has the entire police force working on that. It's no wonder things have gotten so bad."

"If Mr. Narrow finds his daughter, do you think he'd start taking care of the city again?"

"I sure hope he would, but his daughter has been missing for a while now. With missing children, the longer they're gone, the less likely they'll be found. It's already getting close to election day. Even if he were to act now, I doubt it'd be enough."

Upon hearing this, Peggie's mind began to imagine the worst case scenario. *Is it really that Dodie she's talking about? Can she even become mayor? Is it allowed? What is she going to do if she gets that position?* Peggie recalled the surprise visit she and her friends received from the eight-year-old shrew. There's no way someone with that sort of mentality should be given any sort of power.

"Sweetie, are you okay?" her Mom asked, worried by the frightened expression on Peggie's face.

"Huh? Yeah I'm fine ... just a little sleepy is all. When will you be able to come home?" she said to change the conversation.

Her mother smiled. "In a few days I'll be going in for one more checkup, and then I should get the okay."

Peggie brightened up. "I'll be sure to cook you a welcome meal!"

"You don't have to do that."

"But I do! You've been stuck here all this time, eating who knows what. That and ... I really missed you."

Her mother was taken aback by this insistence and finally gave in. "All right, I hope you're good at baking pies."

"Pies?"

"The meal is for me isn't it? Can't I order whatever I want?"

"Sure, whatever you want."

At that moment a doctor wearing his white coat walked into the room, carrying a clipboard in his hands. He looked up from the clipboard and was surprised to see someone else there.

"Oh, is this a bad time?" he asked in a dry, raspy voice.

"No," Ms. Worth said, shaking her head, "did you need something?"

He looked back at his clipboard and adjusted his glasses. "I came here to tell you that the time for your checkup has been pushed up."

Her face brightened up. "Oh, when is it happening?"

He glanced at his clipboard again. "It looks like it'll be in an hour. I'm sorry to have interrupted your conversation."

"It's no problem," Peggie replied. "It just means she can come home sooner, right?" she asked, ecstatic to hear the news.

"If everything checks out, we will release her, yes. We'll be getting ready to examine you, so I suggest you finish up whatever you're discussing."

"You be good now, okay Peggie?" Ms. Worth said.

"Yeah, I will. You get better now, okay?" she replied cheerfully.

"I'm sure I will. See you later!"

With their goodbyes exchanged, Peggie left, feeling like she had won the lottery.

But while Ms. Worth was being briefed on the check-up, she stared at the text message of her phone with a solemn expression. The depressing text read: "I don't think 'us' is going to work out."

Peggie turned down the narrow hallway and toward the nearest elevator. The lack of windows on this trip and the lights overhead made it feel as if she were underground rather than on the second floor of the hospital. At the open area, four elevator doors greeted her.

Peggie pushed the button with the embedded down-pointing arrow, causing one of the lights above the door to illuminate. "Hi!" shouted a voice from behind her, nearly causing her to jump out of her shoes.

"Ah! Who? Jane!" Peggie snapped with irritation at the blurry white mass, which at this point had a hint of black within it.

Jane giggled. "Sorry! I couldn't help myself."

The elevator doors slid open as the bell announced its arrival. Fortunately, no one was in the elevator, so they entered it together.

"So I heard you were visiting your Mom today. Is she ... okay?" Jane opened this can of worms cautiously. Peggie pushed some buttons on the console, the elevator door closed, and she gripped the handle on the wall.

"Yes. She's coming home really soon."

"That's good! Um ... I'm really sorry about all this." Peggie fell silent upon hearing this apology. Jane felt hurt that she said nothing, but Peggie was merely reflecting on the situation. The elevator shook to life and began its descent.

"It's not your fault. It was Janette and Mimi who were responsible for it," she finally answered.

"B-but ... if I hadn't ... if I hadn't brought you into this, then none of it would've happened!" Jane insisted, feeling she deserved to be yelled at.

"It was Janette who made me part of this. If she hadn't attacked me, I would be fine, but she did. Jane, if you hadn't shown up and given me the power to use magic ... I think I'd be dead."

Jane looked away, unsure of how to feel about the situation.

"It's not your fault," Peggie repeated.

The elevator stopped, nearly knocking Peggie off balance. She reached for her cell phone as the elevator door opened and walked out with Jane hovering beside her. They crossed the crowded lobby, continuing their conversation while Peggie pretended to talk into her phone to avoid suspicion.

"I understand if you don't want to do this anymore, Peggie! I'll ... I ... I can find someone else to help."

"No—Janette made it very clear: She won't leave me alone, and ... I'm not sure I trust leaving this to someone else. I mean ... I want to make absolutely sure that the Shadow Carnival goes away. I want to get rid of them because I don't want this to happen again," Peggie asserted, making obvious her hatred for the bizarre circus troupe.

Jane couldn't object to this. "Well, if you're sure." The two of them exited through the doors and into the diesel-scented air outside, on their way to the nearest bus stop.

"Why don't we all get together sometime and hang out?" Peggie proposed, smiling warmly at Jane. "We could learn a bit more about how to use our powers while we're at it!"

"Really?" Jane asked, surprised to hear this.

"Of course really. We all help each other, and I think it's safe to say we're friends now, right?" Peggie replied with a smile.

Jane smiled, too. "Okay! I'll go look for a place where you guys can practice magic! We can like have a base and everything!"

"Good idea—that'll help us out a lot," Peggie replied as they approached the bus stop.

"Definitely, and we can talk about movies and stuff, too, and everyone can do homework together and everything. It'll be fun!" Jane continued to gush with excitement.

"You're really that into movies?" Peggie asked.

"It's my favorite pastime! You know a movie is good when so much heart is put into it. When the environment has so much detail and so do the clothes and makeup. Oh, and when the actors are so into their characters, I can't help but feel like I'm there too with them and everything! What's even more awesome is when the story is just ... so unique! If you put all that together, it's really an amazing experience. I could completely tell you this one scene in a movie where ..." Jane continued this ramble for the rest of the conversation while they waited for the bus to arrive.

CHAPTER 20

Typical Cliffhanger

THE SKY was beginning to be taken over by a shade of orange as evening drew near. However, some business still needed to be done. Dodie was surrounded by a mountain of boxes that littered the yard of the Shadow Carnival.

One of the freaks placed another box down with a sigh of relief. "There, last one!" He smiled as he got ready to dart off.

"Wait!" Dodie commanded, to the freak's disappointment. Dodie looked over the box and wrote a note on her clipboard.

"Mhmm … mhmm … Okay, now I need you to load all these boxes onto the truck we're using to ship them in."

The freak had a horrified look. "B-but I already carried them all."

"You carried them all out of the lab. I need them shipped to the facility we'll be placing our operation in," she said to correct him.

"Can't someone else do that?" he pleaded only to receive a hateful glare.

"All of the others are getting ready for the show. Are you suggesting that you're not willing to work?" she asked, raising an eyebrow.

"Err w-well. It would go faster with more of us. We aren't all staying here, right?" The freak quivered.

"Yes, but I don't want to deal with five of you."

A small cloud of smoke burst into existence and spit out a history book that hovered in the air.

"Now are you going to keep working, or do I have to read you a story?" Dodie said threateningly. The history book opened and turned its pages to the Holocaust section.

"Yes, ma'am. Er ... no, ma'am. Uh ... I ... I'll keep working!" the freak said, stuttering desperately. He returned to work with a faster pace than before. Dodie smiled, pleased with this. Once again adult behavior triumphed over the immaturity of the senseless.

The sight of this freak loading boxes into a truck caught Janette's attention as she entered the lot humming the Shadow Carnival's theme.

"Dodie, are you working on your project again?" Janette asked as she approached the mountain of boxes.

"As a matter of fact, I am. Now the question is: Where have you been?" she replied sternly.

Janette smiled. "Oh, I was off doing stuff."

Dodie's face had a cross expression, "You were slacking off per usual."

"I'm the boss. I make my own work hours. Besides, who says I was slacking?" Janette nonchalantly replied. She began to pry at one of the boxes.

"Don't touch! It's sensitive equipment!" Dodie snapped.

"Oh come on, I just want to see what's in here. Why so secretive?"

"Because it's something that doesn't concern you. I'm sure it would be of no interest to you regardless, so I won't bother explaining," Dodie answered rudely.

"Looks like someone's touchy today!"

"After the way you've been running things ..." Dodie muttered under her breath.

"Huh?" All Janette had heard was mumbling.

"Nothing. Anyway ... I believe there's something we need to discuss."

"Go on." When Janette sat on a pile of boxes they heard the sound of glass breaking. and Dodie glared scornfully.

"I'd prefer it if we could discuss this in private," Dodie said, practically biting her tongue to not yell at Janette for sitting on the boxes.

"Suit yourself." Janette shrugged and followed Dodie into the tent which was abuzz with the laughter and tomfoolery of freakified people practicing their acts. Beyond the chaotic scene, they entered a newly-added section of the tent, a large room with only a cage for animals present in it. The light bulbs that hung overhead dimly illuminated the area.

"So what is it that's got your britches in a knot?" Janette asked casually.

"It's those kids," Dodie began.

"What kids?"

"The ones who put an end to Mimi."

Janette's face lit up. "Oh, *those* kids. What about them? You're not worried are you?"

"Of course not. I just find one of them in particular to be ... interesting."

"Interesting?"

"Yes, that apparition. What was her name? Jane?" Dodie spoke slowly while watching Janette intently. Her expression had changed from her usual nonchalance to one of ... worry?

"You see, I'd like to ask ..."

"I don't know anything. I've never seen her before," Janette said, interrupting.

"Really?" Dodie didn't buy it.

"Yes, really."

"Fine then."

"Actually, Dodie, while we're here I'd like to ask you something. How long have you been running for mayor?"

"I've made an arrangement and pulled some strings. You see, Janette, I'm not really satisfied with my work here at the carnival."

"Oh, you're not?" Janette replied insincerely.

Dodie paced as she spoke, "No. No I'm not. I want more; I deserve more. My talents need to be put to use, and unlike you, I've actually been working hard to get into a position that suits me. Don't fret, though, I'm not leaving the carnival. I'm just going to fix the way things are run here … by taking charge!"

As if she had given a secret signal, a horde of freaks came barreling into the room. Janette was so surprised that she didn't react to being grabbed and lifted into the air. "W-wait! What?" was all she could mutter when Dodie opened the cage door. Janette soon found herself being tossed into the cage and heard the door lock behind her.

"Dodie! What's going on?" Janette asked furiously, finally grasping the situation.

"Simple. A change in management is what's happening," Dodie said. The freaks all cheered.

"Get her!" Janette demanded.

"No can do," one of the freaks answered.

"What? Why?"

"She's the boss!" another answered.

"Yeah, you're just a naughty employee," another freak said, to add to Janette's confusion.

"What? No! *I'm* the boss! I built this carnival. I recruited you. I branded you with my magic. I own you!"

"Ha! She thinks she owns us," said a female freak with a laugh, whereupon the rest of the captors broke out into laughter.

"Huh. That worked better than I thought it would," said Dodie, who smirked and was feeling vastly superior.

"Let's see how your face looks after I burn that smile off!" Janette threatened. She raised her hands … but nothing happened.

"What?" she said with a gasp.

Dodie walked up to the cage, looked Janette straight in the eye, and said, "I'm not entirely sure who or what you are yet, but I've made this cage specifically to deal with you. Now that you're where you belong, I believe it's time I started running this show of yours."

Janette wore a cross expression, "You know … I don't like cages. You just made a very big mistake!"

Dodie's high and mighty response was: "Oh *really* now? You know what? Once my plans fall apart—which they won't because I'm an intelligent adult—I'll let you out of your playpen."

Dodie addressed her posse: "Everyone, let's go! We have work to do."

"What kind of work, Miss Dodie?" one freak asked.

"The kind that'll make the world a better place, of course," she replied. Then she was escorted out of the room while Janette remained and screamed.

"Dodie! Come back here! I'll have your head for this!" she shouted, but Dodie just smirked.

Janette fumed over this turn of events. "You'll regret letting this happen to me!" she threatened.

Jane, who was eaves dropping, was surprised she had been discovered.

"Oh come on—as if I didn't know you were there. I know you're behind this," Janette said.

"Well, you deserved it," Jane replied, approaching hesitantly. "As long you're in that cage, you can't hurt anyone anymore, and I'll finally be rid of you."

"Ha ha!" Janette cackled. "You honestly think that? Oh, how wrong you are! Dodie didn't take *all* of my power away. In fact you're much worse off for it. I'll be certain to make those friends of yours suffer, and you will be powerless to do anything about it—just as you always have been."

"You're bluffing," Jane replied.

"I'm not! You know very well I'm not. You more than anyone should know how I much hate cages. Let me out now, and I'll consider leaving them be," Janette offered, trying to bargain. But Jane backed away as if out of shame.

"Come on. You know this cage won't hold me forever. After all, the last one didn't."

Jane stared at Janette, shook her head, and flew off through the wall. It was apparent that Jane's action left Janette vexed.

"Fine then, run away! Leave me! It's the only thing you're good at. All traitors will pay!" she screamed after Jane.

Janette took a few deep breaths, looked around the room, and examined the cage she was in. Her eyes began to … tear up? Yes, Janette eye's welled up as she curled up into a ball on the floor and began to cry furiously. Her hands curled up into fists, and she swore to herself, "I *will* see this city burn. I will make sure every last one of them burns!"

Printed in the United States
By Bookmasters